Sharon J. Kirk is a chartered surveyor who was born and brought up in Lincolnshire. She is passionate about vintage cars and has published two books of children's stories about *Bitsa, The Vintage Car* with Book Guild Publishing. *Lot 22* is her first book for adults.

Best Wishes
Sharon
29/1/09

LOT 22

Sharon J. Kirk

Book Guild Publishing
Sussex, England

First published in Great Britain in 2009 by
The Book Guild Ltd
Pavilion View
19 New Road
Brighton, BN1 1UF

Typeset in Baskerville by
Ellipsis Books Limited, Glasgow

Printed in Great Britain by
Athenaeum Press Ltd, Gateshead

A catalogue record for this book is available from
The British Library.

ISBN 978 1 84624 301 1

I would like to dedicate this book to my mother, Enid Kirk, and cousin, David Boulton. Thank you both for all your help and patience with the writing of this story.

Also, thank you to all those people who inspired the book — you know who you are. For example the email on page 125, relating to exploding paint, really happened to one of my friends and colleagues, Andrew McGowan.

And to Graham Beckett for his technical knowledge and information relating to the Bugatti Racing Car.

I hope you all enjoy reading this book as much as we enjoyed putting it together.

Part I: The Past

Postcard extract . . .

Dear Benita and young Archie,

Having a successful trip here in Monaco.
Found somewhere nice and safe to store my
belongings. Next trip you must join me.
Our dear friends all thank you for the jars of honey.
See you next week.

Love Archibald
xxxx

1

Monaco in the 1970s

What a coup. The Dandoli family had secured the purchase of a replica Bugatti motor car. Type 35B, green, C8 cylinders, 2,263cc compressor engine – the same as the one with which William Grover (aka Williams), a British National born in 1903, won the first Monaco Grand Prix, in 1929.

A beautiful vintage motor car, this symbol of racing technology stood in the foyer of the Dandoli family's large casino near L'Hotel de Paris. The Dandolis had originated from Venice where they ran small gambling establishments. Some of the family had set up business in Monaco, taking advantage of its attraction to society high-flyers of the day.

Monaco was a grand destination and a favourite of the rich wanting a thrill, wanting to gamble. The Dandoli casino was an ornate affair, full of beautiful red Murano glass.

Archibald Hambleden, a 35-year-old auctioneer from England, was the youngest ever Grand Master of a secret society called The Brotherhood of Members, and he chose to hold their annual general meeting at the casino. He loved Monaco and all it symbolised, and had long been friends with the Dandoli family, who were also members of the society.

Originally a brotherhood of wealthy Bavarian stone craftsmen, The Brotherhood of Members had at that time over five million associates all over the world, some very well-known in public life, including world leaders and celebrities.

Therefore a meeting in Monaco of many of the leading members of the Brotherhood was extremely appropriate. It would be an occasion of glitz and glamour, but the actual proceedings of the meeting itself would be kept very secret.

'Enough publicity to keep us powerful, but giving away very little about our purpose,' thought Archibald.

Archibald's wife, Benita, and young son Archie, stayed at home on this occasion. Archibald had decided, however, that he would bring them both over to Monaco as soon as possible for a holiday. Young Archie was only four, but Archibald thought it only right he should meet his good friends, the Dandolis. After all, they would be a great influence in his life and they were also distantly related to his wife. It was important to Archibald that his son was well aware of his family history, his roots, and sooner rather than later.

Benita, was tall, slim and dark-haired. She was half French, very chic and the perfect wife for Archibald. She supported him in his business and ran their family home, Hambleden Grange, to perfection. She was keen to help the local community, ran charities and helped with local fêtes wherever possible. She was also keen on making her own produce. Her honey and lemon cake, for example, was a particular favourite, being made from her own recipe and using honey from her own bees.

She sold her honey all over the county of Lincolnshire, where the family lived, and even supplied some London stores. People loved it. It seemed to have its own quite unique flavour. When

4

quizzed about it, Benita would just say, 'It's all in the way you look after your bees.' She had a special area of the garden left natural for the bees and around the beehive enclosure she grew the most beautiful plants. These were a bit like tomato plants, though no one quite knew what they were really. Something she must have learnt to grow when she lived in France, people thought. She certainly tended to them regularly, potting them and storing them in her many greenhouses during the frosty months.

'They help the bees,' she would say, 'Happy bees, good honey.' But she would not reveal what they were.

2

Italy 1972

The Black Cats were diamond and jewel thieves. They held a meeting in secret to discuss their latest plans for a theft and transfer. The leader of the group, known as Senior, laid out his ideas to some of his fellow Black Cat Members. He said to them as they gathered round him, 'Pinturicchio was an Italian Painter of the Renaissance period, his dates, 1454 to 1513. He painted *Madonna col Bambino e San Giovannio, Madonna and Child*, in 1486, which is now located in Museo del Duomo – Città di Castello. The painting on wood is screwed to a thin frame. There is no glass to the frame and there is a metal surround forming a display frame. The young girl on the desk is more interested in fashion and make-up and is the only person working in the museum. There is no alarm. The Pinturicchio conservatively is worth about ten million pounds to a collector in today's market. Alternatively, a trade for the authenticity documents of the Doge's Diamonds, some of the most famous diamonds in Italy, could be agreed. In the thirteenth century, Venice, the home of the Doge, became the greatest western commercial power, and thanks to the Doge many diamonds were brought to Antwerp.

'The collector has the documents. He doesn't have the diamonds. He would be happy to trade the Doge's Diamonds authenticity papers for the Pinturicchio. I think we can take the Pinturicchio from the museum, no problem, and get the authenticity documents in return.

The collector is based in Venice.'

'How do you know the documents are genuine?' asked one of the group.

'And . . . who is the collector?' questioned another.

'They are genuine,' said Senior, 'no doubt about that – I have seen them. The collector wishes to be known only as the collector. We must respect his wishes.'

* * *

On 25 September the weather was hot, which was unusual for the time of year in Città di Castello. The Museo del Duomo was a medieval building next to the Umbrian city's cathedral. Carlo had been flirting with the receptionist, Maria, for weeks. Every morning he would take her an espresso and some chocolates or flowers. She didn't like him at first, and thought he was a bit of a Casanova. However, as time went on her feelings changed, and now she couldn't wait to see him each day. He started to bring his paintings and sketches to show her, and she could see that he was very talented. She knew he had little money because the large zip-up art case he brought his paintings in was very worn, but she wasn't bothered, because he made her feel wonderful.

She only had one visitor in the museum that day, an elderly friar. So when Carlo visited, Maria didn't hesitate to sit on the stone step outside the museum with him. He was very charming with his red roses, sparkling eyes and soft, singing voice. He often sang to her, which made her laugh, but she couldn't deny he had a lovely voice. Later he would no doubt show her some more of his paintings, which he had left in his art case at reception while the pair went outside.

The couple talked of their future, and some time later the elderly friar departed. He passed Maria and Carlo on the step, thanking Maria for a lovely visit as he walked towards the city gardens.

Maria was full of excitement. Carlo was truly special she thought, and her future certainly belonged with him. He left soon after the friar, with his art folder. He hadn't shown her any sketches today, and said he had an appointment and had to go, but he would no doubt show her tomorrow.

Maria anxiously waited for Carlo's visit the next day, but he didn't show. She hoped he was all right, that he wasn't ill. He didn't show the next day either, or the one after that – in fact he never returned to the museum again.

Maria never saw him again. Her heart was broken.

* * *

Carlo had spent months and months chatting up the receptionist at the museum in Castello. He began with flowers and chocolate and then slowly started taking paintings and sketches to show her. He needed to take the large art case into the museum regularly, but not look suspicious.

One of his fellow Chat Noir members disguised himself as an elderly friar and while Carlo was with Maria on the steps outside the museum the 'friar' was able to remove the *Madonna and Child* from the museum wall. Surprisingly, nothing was alarmed: an earlier check of the building by other Chat Noir members pretending to be a new cleaning firm preparing a quote for the local authority had enabled them to gain a clear plan of the layout of the museum, and any security issues or nasty surprises were pre-empted. The painting wasn't fastened to the wall very securely: a simple matter of three screws in the back on the metal frame surround. The 'friar' was able to unscrew these easily with a screwdriver he had hidden in a pocket sewn into his costume. Carlo had forged an exact replica of the Pinturicchio, which the 'friar' put in the place of the original. He then carried the original painting back to reception and put it into Carlo's large art folder, said his goodbyes to the courting couple outside, and headed for his car.

He pulled up near the steps of the city wall just behind the city garden, out of view of the museum. Here, Carlo joined him, having said his goodbyes to Maria and collected his art folder before departing.

Back at base, the Pinturicchio was taken out of the art folder and placed into the back of a frame holding a print of *Dora Maar Au Chat* (Dora Maar with Cat), painted in 1941 by Picasso. Carlo and the 'friar' then drove north to Venice along the motorway.

* * *

The collector was delighted with his new painting with its beautiful image of the Madonna, the shape of the work forming a triangle, a great symbol of Renaissance art, and the sign of stability. The dark colours of the subjects' clothes leading to the light on their faces indicated a move from dark to light.

It was quite wonderful, and he didn't hesitate to hand over the authenticity papers of the Doge's Diamonds. The 'friar' checked they were genuine – it was essential that he be certain they were the ones he had seen earlier, and not fakes. Satisfied the pair returned to Castello, only this time out of disguise. Their associate, Andreas, then flew with them to the UK, from Perugia, a very small airport in Umbria, with two planes a week. It was an ex-military airport, but the security guard and dog were not interested in paper – they were looking for drugs, as the area grew much tobacco and was ripe with druggies and dealers alike. The transfer had been easy.

3

Italy 1973

The sun shone through a hole in the wooden shutters of James's flat, which was located on the second floor of a medieval stone building in the Corso, the main street of Castello.

'One day,' he thought, 'I'll be able to afford a flat on the first floor.'

First floor flats, particularly on the Corso Vittorio Emanuele, were very sought after, and always occupied by the rich. Second floor flats were of a lesser quality.

His parents had sent him to Umbria for two or three years so that he could study the art and architecture, which he loved, but also to try and stop his gambling. He had been mixing with the wrong crowd and his gambling had become quite a habit – a debt-forming habit – which he knew he had to stop before it ruined him.

This chance, therefore, to start afresh in such beautiful surroundings was somewhat of a relief to him. A way, he thought, of escaping from himself, of reinventing himself, shutting out the demons of drink, drugs and gambling for good.

He didn't want to let his parents down and would do anything to be a success, to make them proud and prove he was a somebody.

His parents were land-owners and had paid his rent for the apartment for six months. Thereafter, he would have to pay his own way. Anticipating this, he had taken a job in a gallery. He didn't get paid a great deal, and his boss was not particularly pleasant, but he thought it was a good start, and it had stopped his father's enquiries as to why he hadn't bothered to look for work for the first few weeks of his stay in Italy.

'You're not going to act like some wealthy playboy,' his father would say. '*You must get work.*'

Also, he loved art, his favourite painter being Pablo Picasso. And it was through his admiration for Picasso that he had first met Ruth. She passed his gallery most days; it was situated near the Piazza Gabriotti, which contains the central monument of the city, the Cathedral of St Florido. Ruth was very blonde, which surprised him, as it was unusual to see such a fair-haired person in central Italy, particularly one who wore a suit and appeared to be working, not sight-seeing.

One Saturday morning, Ruth walked into the gallery and started to admire the Picasso print of *Dora Maar Au Chat* hanging in the window. It depicted Dora Maar, the painter's Croatian mistress, seated on a chair with a cat sitting on her shoulders. Dora Maar's fingers in the portrait are clawlike. It was a fine example of Picasso's cubic style. Prices had increased rapidly recently, because Picasso had died in April that year.

'Signora, can I help you?' James said to the blonde stranger.

'I just really like the print,' she said. 'Its colours are so vivid; Picasso really was a brilliant man.'

'Yes,' he replied. 'He's my favourite artist.'

'You're English,' she said. 'Unusual to find an Englishman working in Italy.'

12

He laughed. 'Not that unusual. Whereabouts in England are *you* from, signora, or should I say madam?'

'Nottingham, originally. Yourself?'

'Lincolnshire – we're practically neighbours.'

'What brings you to Umbria?' she enquired.

'My family believe it will be good for me to study the art and architecture here. I have a particular interest in this, you see. They want me to gain as much knowledge as I can. They believe it will help me in the future, should I choose to pursue a career in property.'

He thought it wise not to reveal his gambling problem and his parents' hope that a move to Italy would help him get away from the bad company they believed had been influencing him at home.

'You're interested in property?' she replied.

'Fascinating.'

'What about you?' he enquired. 'What brings you to Italy?'

'My husband is Italian,' she said 'We met at university and he was keen to come home to his family. Family is all-important to him, especially now we have young twins of our own.'

'Oh I see,' he said. 'Girls or boys, and how old?'

'A girl and a boy, Millia and Leo, two,' she replied.

'Do you live in Castello then? Only, I've seen you walking past quite regularly.'

'Yes, well, not far, in the area surrounding it. I run an estate agency here, just on the corner of the Corso; that's why I was so interested in your comment about your intentions to consider a job in property.'

'Small world,' he replied. 'Well, at the risk of being too forward, if you're ever looking for staff I hope you will remember me.'

'Yes, I will,' she said. 'I will.'

The gallery door opened and in walked a very dark, short,

sulky Italian. He had curly hair and was with two young children in a dual pushchair. He mumbled something in Italian.

'Yes, yes,' replied the woman, announcing him. 'This is my husband, Vincenzo. I'm sorry, he wants to go. I must go also. Listen, I may have a position for you in my firm, I'll speak to you next week. Are you here next week? I'll drop in.'

'Yes,' he replied, 'every day.'

'What's your name?' she enquired.

'It's James, my name is James,' he said.

James, he thought. I definitely want to be known as James. My fresh start, starts here.

'I'm Ruth,' she said.

4

Italy 1974

The Upper Tiber valley is in the northernmost Umbrian territory. It has always been in close cultural and social contact with the neighbouring regions of Tuscany and the Marches. The River Tiber runs through the entire length of the valley for fifty kilometres, bestowing great fertility on the soil, which is intensely farmed for tobacco. The area comprises eight townships: Città di Castello, Citerna, Lisciano Niccone, Montone, Monte Santa Maria Tiberina, Pietralunga, San Giustino and Umbertide.

James's father had spent a lot of his youth in the area. His family had been farmers for generations and having completed some of his National Service in Italy, he had returned to study the region's farming methods. In many ways the fertile soil was similar to that at James's family farm. His father thought it sensible therefore to send his son to this area. Hopefully he would appreciate the beautiful location and it would help to tame his wild ways.

James had started his job with Ruth in her estate agency within two weeks of their first meeting. He had a real knack for selling houses and being a 'proper charmer'. As a result his sales rate was phenomenal. Ruth was very impressed.

As the demands of her family ever increased, her relationship with her husband Vincenzo worsened. His gambling and drinking seemed to get more and more extreme. She relied more and more on James.

After a year Ruth made James a junior partner in the business. He became a good friend to her and she confided her problems to him.

The estate agency at least was doing well for her. It was this and the success James had brought to the firm together with the joy her children gave her that kept her going.

It was a rainy Tuesday morning in November 1974. James found Ruth in her office with her head in her hands. She was in tears, just visible below her dark glasses. He put his arm round her to comfort her. She flinched as though he had hurt her. He pushed her jacket sleeves up and saw that her arms were black and blue.

Defeated now, she removed her dark glasses, revealing a black eye. Her face was swollen.

'Oh my God,' said James. 'What on earth has happened to you? I mean, my God! Have you been mugged?'

'No,' Ruth replied. 'It's Vince. He's always been volatile, but lately his temper has got worse. Fuelled with drink and drugs, well, he's becoming very violent. Accusing me of all sorts. It's as though the drugs and drink are feeding his insecurities about me. Totally unfounded, I don't know what's got into him. He hasn't, thank God . . .' her voice began to falter. 'He hasn't turned on the children, but, well, I am worried. Very very worried.'

'That's awful,' said James. 'Truly awful.' He was truly shocked, horrified at what he saw. He regained control of his composure and, wiping tears from his eyes, said, 'You can't possibly carry on like this, Ruth. You need to get away.'

'It's not that easy!' she cried. 'James, it's just not that easy.'

'I'll help you in any way I can,' he said. 'Any way I can, should you change your mind. Think about it, you must be able to get away.'

5

Things went from bad to worse for Ruth and Vince. His mood swings became more frequent and more violent. He was full of remorse after each event, swearing it would never happen again. But of course it did happen again. It happened over and over again.

In the end Ruth knew she had to get away from Castello. But how? She would never leave her children, but Vince would never let them go. Especially not his precious son, his heir, Leo. In total despair, she sat in her study in her large three-storey house on the outskirts of Castello, drinking brandy. She and her family lived on the outskirts of Vince's family farm. Theirs was a nice house, built of pinkish stone, excavated from the neighbouring town of Spello. There was a white dust road leading to the house, which also had a swimming pool. Vince's family were wealthy land-owners, although over the years their land had dwindled. Theirs had been a fortune based on tobacco farming and trade, but increasingly they relied on government subsidy. They often had to sell an estate house to pay off Vince's ever increasing gambling debts.

'Come on,' she said to herself, 'don't you start drinking as well. He'll drag you down to his level. Think about the children.'

She tipped her head back in her swivel chair, put her feet on her desk and shut her eyes. If only she could sleep. She hadn't really had a good sleep for months. She was frightened and didn't know what she would wake up to. She grabbed the odd hour here and there, even in the office.

Vince was out, the children were safe at school. For a brief while she could try to rest, at least close her heavy, sore eyes.

She looked up at the wall, and saw her prize possession – a beautiful painting of Lincoln cathedral in England. She sat up in her chair with a start. She had had an idea. She felt relief and hope; was it possible, was it possible? It must work. It was her only hope.

6

Five months later, five further months of hell, it was six o'clock in the morning and Vince had arrived home in a drunken state as usual. He had called Ruth into the kitchen. 'Espresso, espresso *now!*' he kept yelling. He flung himself on the leather sofa near the window as he always did, belching, farting and swearing – as he always did. A creature of habit. A vile, angry creature of habit.

Ruth took him his espresso. He snatched it from her, and she flinched. He just stared at her and laughed.

'Thirsty – more coffee woman, more, *more!*' He stood up and smacked her across the face. 'Espresso *now!*' he yelled.

She gave him a large mug of coffee this time, and brought the whole pot as well.

Her face hurt where he had hit her, and she fought back the tears. 'The bastard,' she thought, 'the bastard.'

Composing herself she said, 'Here we go darling, I've brought you a pot of coffee this time, that way you can drink as much as you need.'

'Pour it then,' he snarled, 'Come on, come on, you lazy cow, *pour* it!'

She did as she was told. It took two more pots of coffee, six mugs in all, until he finally shut his eyes. She checked his pulse; still beating but faint. She didn't want to kill him, just ensure he remained fast asleep for at least twenty-four hours. Enough time for her and the children to get away from this foul monster. Coffee and sleeping pills should constitute a nice cocktail that would keep Vince, already full of alcohol, out of her hair for a good while.

She crept upstairs, careful not to wake Vince. Logic said he wouldn't wake, not yet, but she couldn't take any risks. The children were in bed, and she pulled their covers back. They were fully dressed, ready for the journey.

They all crept past Vince, still sprawled fast asleep on the sofa in the lounge. She knew he was alive – his farting and snoring were regular and loud.

'Quietly children,' she whispered. 'We don't want to wake Papa now, do we? You know how he doesn't like being woken up.'

They were to go on a great adventure, she had told the children. A great and wonderful new adventure. They could take only a few possessions with them. She carried a small rucksack with mostly things for the children and their teddy bear and doll.

They walked quickly down the drive, soon breaking into a run. At the bottom of the hill a small three-wheeled truck picked them up. Ruth and the children had to lie in the back, covered with sheeting, so as not to be spotted. The driver's cab was too small to hold them all. In fact, the driver filled the cab. She knew he was genuine. He produced a card of a black cat as proof. The truck took them to a car outside the walls of the old town. A tall slim man with grey hair stood by the side of the car.

'Thank you for the painting of Lincoln cathedral,' he said. 'I will look after it, I promise.'

She helped him strap the children in his car.

'I'll meet you in one hour,' he said, 'at the train station in the city of Arrezzo. Don't be late. You must not be late.'

'No I won't,' she said.

She gave her children a kiss, told them to be good and that she wouldn't be long. They were not to be frightened, he was a nice man. A friend of Mama's. Wiping a tear from her eye she ran to her office, thinking about the weeks of planning that had led to this point.

* * *

Some weeks before she had travelled to Rome to the British embassy, going by car from Castello along the motorway south, telling her husband she was going on a business trip, which James had verified as Vince did not trust her. She met with the British ambassador, Mr Sporton, the same man she had just left her children with. She explained her problems with her husband and asked for help.

He was very sympathetic, but at first unable to offer her help or indeed any satisfactory solution to her problem. However, when she showed him a photograph she had taken of her Lincoln cathedral painting she had had hung in her study for so long, his tone changed.

He agreed to help her, but first he must have the painting to confirm its authenticity. Ruth stayed in Rome for several more days and arranged for one of her staff to drive the painting to her hotel. Vince didn't realise what was going on, and in any case was far too drunk to care.

Ruth returned to the embassy with the painting. She was struck at how beautiful but ordered the building was. Security was very tight. The painting was screened and the frame checked several times before she was allowed to see the ambassador with it.

An armed guard led her and the painting along the marble-floored corridor and up the ornate stairs to the ambassador's office. It still impressed her even though she had made this journey only two days earlier.

The ambassador dismissed the guard and took the painting from the brown packaging it had been wrapped in. The packaging was loose as it had already been removed once for the embassy security teams to check.

'Sit down my dear,' the ambassador said as he examined the painting with a magnifying glass. He smiled. He knew it was genuine. Ruth knew then *he* was genuine. He gave her a small card, with a black cat on it, a similar image to that of the *Chat Noir*, the black cat painted by the artist Toulouse Lautrec.

'Keep this always, my dear,' he said. 'This is your passport out of here. This is your passport to a new and hopefully better future.'

* * *

She smiled to herself as she remembered how relieved she had felt when he said this to her. She pulled herself back to reality, back to the escape – she had very little time. Now she must act fast. She arrived at her office and went inside.

7

It was still early, the office had not yet opened. Her staff had not yet arrived. She went to her desk, where the contract was waiting. James had signed his half. Ruth signed hers. Good old James, she thought, a true friend, always there for her.

James had agreed to help Ruth in any way he could. He had been horrified at the batterings Vince had given her time and time again, shocked at the life she had been forced to lead. He had told Ruth that his father had provided him with some money to set up home in Italy and he was going to use some of this to buy Ruth out of her business. He had agreed to arrange for the money to be transferred into an account in England which she had had set up for her by the embassy, so that no documentation could be found at her house by Vince or his family. She was to sign the contract of sale this morning, pre-witnessed. Not altogether ethical, but she trusted James and James trusted her. That she felt sure. All was done.

She would now make her way to the train station in Arrezzo, and a train would take her and her children to Rome. There, using false identities, they would fly out of Rome. Anyone pursuing them would not know where to find them.

A scooter driver pulled up outside the office, tooted and showed her his card. The card had an image of a black cat on it. She opened the door and showed him her black cat card.

'Just give me one minute,' she said. 'I'll be with you in one minute.'

She felt quite emotional as she took one last look around her office. Her estate agency that she had built up from nothing. People had been sceptical, a foreign woman expecting to make a success of business, who did she think she was? But she had made a success of herself. Now she was going to leave it all behind. Her children and safety came first, every time. She smiled as she thought how she would be able to start again with the money James was paying her for her share of the business. Enough for a decent house, not too over the top, but comfortable, and a nice office. Start small, she thought, then expand from there.

Her daydream was abruptly interrupted by the ringing of her fax machine. She waited until the fax had spewed out all the documents, just to make sure it was not a warning message for her.

She read the fax. She felt numb. She collapsed into a chair. The tears rolled down her cheeks, and she wept uncontrollably. She could hardly move. She felt sick.

She had no choice now. She knew she had to leave, but why did he do this to her? What sort of life were her children going to have now?

The man on the scooter waiting for her outside tapped on the window. He signalled at his watch that really she ought to move, time was short.

She left the office, drained and deflated, and sat on the back of the scooter. She put a helmet on, held on to the driver and shut her eyes.

'I've got to be strong,' she thought, 'for the children. I've got to pull myself together, come on girl, think of the children.'

8

Ruth joined her children at the train station on the outskirts of Arrezzo. Arrezzo was a much larger city than Castello. It was the central trading area of the region and home to one of the country's leading antique fairs. A tall, slim, dark-haired man was waiting for her. He showed her his card of the black cat. The children were with him they looked pleased to see Ruth, not really sure whether they still liked playing this game.

Ruth held her children tight and closed her eyes, to try to hold back the tears – they must not see her crying. They must not know she was upset. They must certainly not know she was frightened.

Ruth and her children were ushered by the man into the cargo compartment of the train leaving for Rome. A second man, smaller than the first, younger, with a long moustache, showed her the compartment. He spoke English. He was very cheerful and comforting. He handed Ruth his black cat card.

'I will be in the porter carriage just behind your cargo area,' he said.

He handed her and the children some blankets, gloves, some bread rolls and some rum for Ruth and orange juice for the children.

26

'You will need these,' he said. 'Very cold journey.'

He secured the side of the cargo area, and soon Ruth could feel the train start to move.

'Mama, Mama,' said her little girl, Millia, 'I'm scared of the dark, I want to go home. I don't want to play adventures any more, I want my dolls' house instead now please.'

'In a while, I promise,' said Ruth. 'I promise we will be home and we can play with your dolls' house.'

'Dolls are for girls,' said Leo. 'I hate dolls, I'm not playing with her silly dolls' house. Sissy, sissy, afraid of the dark, sissy, sissy, sissy.'

'I'm not a sissy!' said Millia. 'I'm not, I'm not, I'm not, tell him Mama, tell him I'm not a sissy.'

'That's enough, children,' said Ruth, fighting a headache. 'Close your eyes now, try to rest.'

'Mama, Mama,' said Millia. 'It smells in here, oh it really smells.'

'I know darling,' Ruth said. She wasn't sure what cargo the train was carrying, it was dark, and she couldn't make out the contents of the load. She had to agree with her daughter though, whatever it was, it was pretty vile.

9

What seemed like hours of rumbling wheels, a vile smell and crying children followed. Ruth felt empty: full of despair and very very sick. She wasn't sure whether her sickness was brought on through shock, the vile smell of the cargo compartment of the train, fear, or motion sickness. For the first time in her life she didn't know what she was going to do. She had no plan, no idea what was to become of her and her children.

The cheerful train attendant she had spoken to earlier opened the door from his porter carriage.

'Mama, Mama,' cried Millia, 'I want to go home, I'm scared.' Ruth clung tight to her children, she felt weary herself, what was happening?

The attendant told her and the children to move as far back to the end of the carriage as they could. They must remain underneath their blankets and not make a sound. They were about to enter the cargo clock in bay. If they were found they would be in serious trouble. The children would almost certainly be returned to their father. She couldn't have that happen, not after all she'd risked, all she'd sacrificed. The three lay silent beneath their blankets. 'Now children,' she said, 'it is important you don't move and don't make a sound.'

The guards checked the cargo documentation and then with the attendant opened the cargo carriage. One shone his torch across its vile smelling cargo. Coughing and holding his nose, he soon shut the door. The train attendant gave him and his fellow guard four beers, which he had vigorously shaken before reaching the control area. 'That'll teach the bastards,' he thought, smiling to himself. The guards smiled at their gift of beer and soon let the train pass without any further checks or questions.

Ruth could feel her heart thumping; she thought it was going to beat out of her chest. She held onto her children's hands. She could feel their pulses racing also. 'God,' she thought, 'we've got to come through this, we've just got to.'

* * *

Antonio, the cheerful train cargo attendant, sat in his small office at the back of the train. He was nervous; he hoped they wouldn't check his cargo any more – spot checks were common in Italy, with too many different types of police trying to justify their existence, and he didn't think a few beers would be enough to satisfy all of them.

'Please,' he thought, 'please God.' He wanted to return home to Perugia as soon as possible, his wife and children would be waiting. He knew though he had to help the ambassador. He had to help those with the black cat calling card.

What an honour to be carrying a black cat card. Nerves gave way to pride just for a few moments.

Antonio returned to Ruth and the children to check they were all right. 'Ruth,' he whispered, 'Ruth?'

Ruth's small head appeared over the blanket and was just recognisable in the torchlight.

'Nearly there,' Antonio said. 'We're nearly there. I've brought you some more drink and food. Eat up, but stay hidden under the blanket, nice and quiet. Be ready to move in about twenty minutes, when I tell you. We will reach the station in Rome. This carriage sticks out of the station, being at the back. My colleagues will uncouple it. It has its own power; a small electric engine for moving around stations. It will be moved to another siding. Then I will let you out of the carriage. You should run to the parked trains to the left. You will be helped from there.'

'Mama,' said Leo, 'I want the toilet.'

'Me too,' said Millia, 'me too.'

'Children, quickly now,' said Ruth, 'Go to the toilet in the corner.'

'Err,' said Millia, 'that's horrible, that's . . .'

'I know,' said Ruth. 'Just this once you will have to go in the corner of the carriage.'

They made their way around the large crates of cargo. Still Ruth could not make out what the cargo was; the smell didn't improve though. All three of them went to the toilet in the corner of the carriage. As she crouched down, Ruth realised what the cargo was, and she didn't want the children to see. She ushered them carefully back to their blankets, fighting back her sick.

The train stopped and Ruth and the children were let out of the cargo carriage by Antonio. He wished them luck and Ruth ran, holding her children's hands, to the parked carriages as Antonio had instructed her. She was met by a man holding a black cat card. He ushered the three weary travellers into the back of a laundry truck.

The truck took them to the main airport in Rome, Fiumicino. They went into the laundry room of a large hotel on the outskirts of the airport. A short, grey-haired lady met them there, gave them some clean clothes and the three had a chance to have a

30

bath and freshen up. Then they were taken out of the front of the hotel and met at the entrance by a large black car. The driver showed them his black cat card and gave them their new identity cards, which in Italy also act as passports. The car then took them to the VIP lounge of the airport and they successfully boarded a plane to the UK. Ruth felt scared when she passed passport control, but the officer was more interested in flirting with her than checking her identity card.

The three sat on the plane waiting for take-off. Millia was a bit scared, Leo very excited.

'Try to sleep now, children,' said Ruth, 'try to sleep.'

Ruth closed her eyes. She would miss Italy, the country she now called home – the beautiful frescoes of Assisi, the pinkish stone of Spello which she had used in her own house. She remembered when she first visited Castello, with its tall houses and narrow streets, large chestnut doors and ornate door knockers; how excited about her future she had been back then; what a mistake to make.

*   *   *

The plane landed at Heathrow, and the three travellers passed through passport control relatively quickly.

Ruth felt scared and tired, relieved and sad, all at once. She knew this journey had ended, they were safe, but she wondered what their next journey, their next adventure, would turn out like. She felt churned up as she thought of Vince back in Italy. He would be well awake now, frantic and angry. She felt hurt and betrayed when she thought of James – how could he? How could he? The bastard. Someday she thought, someday he will pay.

She was left with nothing – she had to build herself up, rebuild her confidence. She knew she would never be the same again though – never be able to trust again. This sort of thing didn't happen in real life. James was only young and some would say she had been naïve to take him on, but she thought they were friends – she never dreamt anyone would do that to her, not when they knew the full facts about her history. She had given him his start in Italy, in business for God's sake.

* * *

'Mrs Fizzellii,' said Chief Inspector Flynn, walking towards Ruth in the airport arrivals lounge. 'You're safe now, we will house you and your young son and daughter in a hostel until you get back on your feet.' He passed her a postcard with a picture of a black cat on it, and she knew he was genuine.

10

The trio's start in the UK was not easy to say the least. Thanks to James they were left with no money. They were living on the breadline, very different to their lifestyle back in Italy. Ruth had to buy clothes for her and the children from charity shops.

She hated Vince, but she hated James even more for what he had done to her. She didn't miss the terrible time Vince had given her during their marriage, but she missed Italy.

On occasion her new-found poverty was so great she wondered whether it had all been worth it. But then she would remember Vince's violence – thank goodness he never hit the children, but if he had, what then? She couldn't have taken the risk. She resolved to carve out a new life and work her way back to the lifestyle she knew she deserved. The lifestyle she wanted for her children. If she didn't make a success of the UK, then the struggle to escape would have been a waste of time.

She remembered how she had travelled, unbeknown to Vince, to Sansepolcro, a neighbouring town of Castello. She went to the cathedral there to provide another black cat contact with photographs of her and her children for their new identity papers. She remembered the cathedral well. She had visited it many times before. It was constructed in the eleventh century as a church in

Romanesque style, and was dedicated to St John the Baptist. Having been damaged by an earthquake in 1352, the town was redeveloped, and the church was expanded to its present size. In 1515, Sansepolcro became a diocese and as a consequence the church became a cathedral. Later the style of the building was transformed into Baroque. Only in the last thirty years had it been restored to its original appearance. She always loved the building, in fact her children were christened there. How elaborate the christening had been; how different her life was now. She never dreamt when she passed her photographs through the priest's curtain in the confessional booth that her journey would end like this, with such hardship. She cried as she thought of the beautiful cathedral, with its frescoes by the school of Romangio representing the Virgin, with St Catherine of Alexandra and St Thomas a Becket, and the two statues of Saints Benedetta and Romuldo by the School of Della Robbia, protected by panes of glass positioned inside the façade. What could she do? What could she have done? Yes, she would get her status back. Yes, one day her children would be safe to return to Italy, heads held high. One day she would get revenge on James – *most definitely*.

11

James sat in the gambling club in the basement of the market café. He smiled to himself as he puffed on his large cigar and drank some wine. Where did Ruth think he was going to get that sort of money from? How naïve she had been.

Now though, he had the money, he had the whole estate agency business. He was a success. He just had to curb his gambling. Still, he thought, the odd flutter didn't do anyone any harm. Besides which, he decided not to gamble for money any more – instead he would gamble for items of worth.

James always seemed to win his bets, much to the distaste of Andreas Dandoli, the gambling club owner. Still, thought Andreas, if you wanted a risky job doing, perhaps James was your man.

Vince, of course, was also a gambler. It had been easy to encourage him to increase his time gambling, increase the risks he took. He was a weak man, easy to lead astray. First Vince's drinking increased, then James introduced him to 'wacky backy', slowly feeding him stories of Ruth's odd behaviour. Drunk and full of drugs and jealousy, Vince was convinced Ruth was having an affair. James made Vince insecure, filled his head full of lies, the demons of insecurity and fear. James knew all about these, he had had similar fears back in England, similar problems until his family sent him to Italy for a fresh start.

Now he was in control. The odd cigar, the odd spliff, the odd snort, a few bottles of wine – where was the harm in that, he thought. The stories he made up about Ruth for Vince were brilliant. He regretted seeing her bruises, but he learnt how to block these from his mind. His goal had always been to get her business, her wealth and her lifestyle.

*   *   *

Vince never got over his family leaving him. There was a local police search of course, but they were never traced. Officials seemed to block Vince's every move. James, his friend, had said he would help him drown his sorrows. He looked after him, gave him pills, cigarettes and money for drink. He said it was the least he could do. He even took care of Ruth's business for her, for her return.

'Sad git that Vince,' thought James, 'sad silly git, I'll keep him sweet for a while, I'll pay his debts for him, and in return I'll take his lovely house off his hands.'

Vince's situation got worse and worse. He drank and drank and became sadder and sadder. His family disowned him, the authorities were not interested in his sorry tale of his missing wife and children. As soon as he mentioned his name, they seemed to switch off. Eventually, when he had no more money, no more furniture or property to trade, James, his best friend, also disowned him; totally ignored him. Vince vanished.

12

Italy 1977 – Magazine article, *Valley Life*

Following a series of robberies that have hit the Niccone Valley and its environs, we are publishing here the letter of a heartbroken English citizen to the British Consulate and other authorities. This scourge of summer break-ins affecting houses in the country is very upsetting, given the vastness of the region, which makes it difficult to put a stop to them. It is an ever-increasing problem that cannot be tolerated.

Dear Sir,

I write further to our recent telephone conversation. I am a British citizen, I have spent three months in the country learning the Italian language and touring. During my stay near Lisciano Niccone in the Val Niccone on the borders of Umbria and Tuscany, I have been subjected to a terrible ordeal. The Val Niccone is suffering an unprecedented crime wave and as a victim of two separate incidents within the last few weeks, I feel that I must make the authorities aware of the growing concern and possible scenarios that are arising from this unfortunate situation. Clearly I do not have access to official data, however, I would conservatively estimate that Val Niccone has seen in excess of thirty minor/serious incidents of housebreak-ins, in the last six weeks. These break-ins are affecting Italians, English, Americans and Germans, that I know of. The break-ins have included serious theft such as cars and high value equipment. I myself awoke to find a burglar at the foot of my bed. He escaped, but I would recognise him in a line-up, his piercing eyes and moustache. The police are making enquiries but I am quite traumatised at the break-ins and have lost a small gold brooch of a cat with diamond eyes, which my husband gave me for our first wedding anniversary. On another occasion, the area around Preggio suffered seven separate incidents in one night.

Clearly such events are leading to a reaction from local residents and from conversations with friends and locals of all nationalities, it is quite clear that people are now choosing to protect themselves in a variety of ways unprecedented in this area. I have been party to conversations where individuals have spoken about the possible use of firearms which they own. Despite the above we fail to see any real reaction from the authorities. I am fully aware of the social and economic pressures under which the authorities operate, but it is quite clear that this area is being targeted and therefore it would be reasonable to expect counter-measures from the authorities. I feel the problem is due to the fact that the area is managed by so many different authorities, Lisciano, Niccone, Umbertide, Citti di Castello and Cortona. There is no coordination or collaboration between these areas.

I would be grateful for your assistance in sorting this matter out. I am quite distressed and at the moment feel scared to go out.

Yours faithfully
Benita Hambleden (Mrs)

James read the article and laughed. Silly woman, she would not recognise him again in a crowd, he was sure of that. Daft bat, she woke just as he passed the bottom of her bed, she must have

38

seen his shadow in the bright moonlight. She claims she is distressed, and it was a shock for him also – she looked like something out of a horror film in her rollers, hairnet and night face cream. He thought the owners were away, didn't think she'd be there.

He'd recognise her again, but if he ever saw her he would be discreet. She wouldn't recognise him, wouldn't realise, though perhaps he would shave off his moustache, cut his long curly hair really really short. He was starting to go bald anyway.

He would soon leave Italy, go back home to the UK, to Lincolnshire. He was bored now with Umbria.

He smiled as he looked at the golden brooch with diamond eyes, street value, say two million pounds. A good night's work he thought.

Part II: The Present

Dear Archie,
All organised with this electronic mail communication system
now. Very pleased. Mum asks whether you want to come for tea?
Your father.

Reply . . .

Thanks Dad, you know you could have come to my office to
ask this, as we work in the same building; email is to help
you not to stop you mixing with everyone.
Archie.

13

Lincolnshire 2006

Hambleden Garings, established in 1833, auctioneers and estate agents. Archibald Reginald Lawrence Hambleden, Archie to his friends, was a tall, thin chap with dark hair. He was the senior partner of the practice. A bachelor, he lived in a large house with his housekeeper Mrs Pearl and his black cat called Lautrec, after the painter.

Archie lived with the burden of having to find a wife and produce a son and heir for the family business – a long line of estate agents and auctioneers, all with the family name, Archibald.

Archie's father, Mr Archibald Lawrence Hambleden, Mr Hambleden senior to his friends, had often retired from the family firm. He was in his early seventies, but could not resist spending at least two or three days a week at the office, interfering with the office structure, proving to himself and all who would listen that the human brain was far more efficient and accurate than any damn silly computer.

His office was located on the ground floor of the building, close to reception and was full of antiques, photographs and all his retirement presents – a clock, a pen, golf clubs, you name it, all lovingly bought from collections given by the Hambleden Garings loyal staff, and presented to Mr Hambleden on a Friday as he waved goodbye, leaving the office in the capable hands of his son, only to return the following Tuesday morning, bored and much to the relief of his long suffering wife. His latest retirement present was a Tom Tom satnav system. This was proving difficult for Mr Hambleden senior to understand. Despite his protests ('Technology? Who needs technology?'), Mr Hambleden senior was quite taken with the satnav and although he couldn't work it he carried it around with him all over. 'Just humouring the staff,' he would say in public, although everyone knew he was secretly pleased with it.

Ronald Garings was Archie's business partner, a small man with blondish hair, balding on top, with trendy glasses, chosen by his wife Kitty, a bossy redhead with ideas of social standing way above her station. They had a daughter called Molly, seven, going on seventeen. 'With her mother's personality and father's looks she'll have a tough life,' thought Archie.

Ronald was an annoying little chap, but very loyal to Archie and his father and rather a good estate agent. His assistant, Timothy Cromwell, helped him with his duties as estate agent/ office manager. A retired army officer, he went about life in the estate agency with much order, and liked to make lists.

With Maggie and Lily in reception, Mrs Limb the office secretary (who everyone knew really ran the firm), Graham Pening, the office accountant and letting agent and several others who will be introduced later, that about makes up the Hambleden Garings office team. In addition there was, though, Sidney Trust, a rather strange and smelly young lad, who used to help Archie at the cattle market on a Thursday morning and at monthly auctions, and was also responsible for office maintenance and

44

sometimes office junior duties. Sidney obviously didn't like the idea of washing and would have made the ideal Bisto Kid, on account of his vapour trail.

14

The cattle market was a loss-making venture Archie ran every Thursday for the local farmers, a long-standing tradition, followed by his father and his father before him. It was a joint venture with 'Hewton and Terry', a spin-off estate agency firm originally part of a steady chain of estate agents, 'Terry's', which had slowly reduced in size with parts bought out by the various partners. Much to Archie's distaste, the Lincolnshire office had been taken over by Vernon Hewton (known as Vermin in the profession), who had renamed it Hewton and Terry (known as Tom and Jerry in the profession, because it was widely regarded as a Mickey Mouse outfit).

Although partners in the cattle market there was much rivalry between the firms in their estate agency and other property related departments and both senior partners much enjoyed wining the upper hand over each other. Vernon Hewton thought Archie 'A devious cocky little shit – that one lives by the sword and will die by the sword – not giving a monkeys whom he hurts to get what he wants.'

A good example of Archie and Vernon's rivalry occurred at one of the cattle markets. Archie was quite annoyed with Sidney because he kept standing in front of the tag machine as the cattle were paraded around the ring. The tag machine would indicate which lot number the cow was part of and allow Archie (the auctioneer for the day) to read out the lot detail.

After several 'move out of the way please Sidneys' Archie got cross, because although Sidney heard him he seemed not really to move very far from the tag machine, still restricting Archie's view.

In the end Archie said at the top of his voice, (forgetting he had left the microphone on), 'WILL YOU MOVE OUT OF THE BLOODY WAY SIDNEY!' This much amused the audience of farmers and buyers, but not half as much as Vernon's comments.

He turned to Archie and at the top of his voice and still with the microphone on, said, 'GOD ARCHIE, YOU DON'T HALF EMPLOY SOME RIGHT DICKHEADS IN YOUR FIRM.'

Such comments left the market in hysterics and that afternoon Archie went home to bed to try to deal with his migraine, clearly brought on by distress caused by the cattle market fiasco.

This, together with the fact that on his way to market Mr Hambleden senior had lost one of his cows. He had it hooked behind the car on a trailer. Somehow the hook had not worked properly and Mr Hambleden's now detached cow and trailer had overtaken him on the way to market. The trailer hit such a high speed going downhill that it triggered a speeding camera. Everyone felt sure that the photograph of 'speeding cow on trailer' would most definitely feature in the national papers. Typical, thought Archie.

Vernon Hewton couldn't resist taking the mickey out of Archie about it, asking him if he could arrange to get the cow's autograph. He suggested that at the next market they should sell the cow with autographed speeding ticket and photograph. That should up its sale price.

Thus there was not much love lost between Hambleden Garings and Hewton and Terry, not much at all.

15

In addition to the cattle market, Hambleden Garings ran a monthly auction of chattels, usually old bits of rubbish and furniture that seemed to go round the auction circuit month by month, passed from buyer to seller, seller to buyer, time and time again.

Every so often however, the firm ran an antiques auction, where they would produce a catalogue. It was the morning of the catalogue auction, and Archie and Ronald were preparing to officiate alternately so that neither would lose their voice. Graham Penning was booking in. Lily and Mrs Limb were packing the items once sold. Sidney was helping the team of experienced freelance porters who would walk around the auction house highlighting or carrying items, depending on their weight.

All electrical items were tested prior to sale and each porter had to read out details of the test certificate to the audience when instructed by Archie. All except Sidney, who since he had made a fool of himself at the last auction was instructed to stay silent. At the last auction Archie had asked Sidney to read out the test certificate details on an electric blanket, and he misinterpreted the instruction and shouted out to the audience, 'Er er um, it er says er, "Warning".' This proved yet another source of humiliation to Archie, but a further source of amusement to the general public. 'Still,' Archie thought to himself, 'he *is* cheap.'

Hambleden Garings were not renowned for being good payers. More the other way in fact. 'Archie Hambleden,' people would say, 'nice chap but has short arms and deep pockets.' Mr Hambleden senior was exactly the same, and often he would use old property papers in his outside toilet back at Hambleden Grange, much to the surprise of many a garden party guest.

*   *   *

'No, no, no,' cried a tall, thin woman with dark hair at Mrs Limb at the item dispensary. 'I bought Lot 22 – see, it says in the catalogue, a painting of Lincoln cathedral by R.J. Langton. This is clearly not a painting but a print of a lady in a cubic style with a black cat on her shoulder. Its called *Dora Maar au Chat* I think, done by Picasso and it's not a very clear print at that.'

'What's the matter?' asked Archie as he passed by.

Mrs Limb explained the problem.

'Oh, oh really,' said Archie. 'The painting was withdrawn from the sale. We replaced it with this Picasso print. I can't see why therefore you have been misled today as the painting is no longer here.'

'I left a bidding slip yesterday,' said the lady.

'Oh, oh really,' said Archie. 'I asked Sidney to call all pre-bidders to tell them of the lot change, did he not ring you?'

'No.'

'*Sidney*!' Archie shouted. 'Why didn't you call this lady yesterday with the lot change details?'

'Oh er, um er, sorry,' mumbled Sidney. 'I, er, well, forgot.'

Archie was cross, but maintained his composure and agreed

to put the Picasso print back into the auction, not charging the lady.

'Thank you,' she said, but started to cry.

'Oh, now, what's the matter?' asked Archie, feeling awkward, not comfortable dealing with people's tears.

'Its just that painting was done by my great-great grandfather,' said the lady.

'R.J. Langton was your great-great grandfather?' said Archie. 'How fascinating.'

'Well yes,' she said, 'I was thrilled to see it in the catalogue and just knew I had to have it, but now . . .' She wept. 'Sorry, I'm all emotional. Well, never mind I'll just have to forget it.'

'Well, not necessarily,' said Archie. 'I know the owner very well. I'll see him tomorrow, and I could ask him, if you would like, whether he would be pleased to sell it after all.'

'Oh, would you?' replied the lady. 'Oh wonderful, thank you.'

She left her details with Archie, who found he was quite taken with her: Emilia Langton, art collector and dealer, staying at the Arlington Arms hotel, on the high street.

16

Armond Hall was a large seventeenth-century manor house, boasting thirty bedrooms, two stately dining halls and numerous study and reception rooms. It lay in the heart of the Lincolnshire Wolds with land stretching over eight hundred acres, being of mixed farm, grass and woodland.

Lord Armond was an elderly gent and a confirmed bachelor. He divided his time between Armond Hall, which he shared with his housekeeper, Mrs Temple, and visits to London to see his sister and her family.

Hambleden Garings had for many generations looked after the accounts and estate for the Armond family, much to the envy of Vernon Hewton, who often tried to woo Lord Armond, showing off the services of the ultra-modern Hewton and Terry, but Archie was confident, although not complacent, that for the time being at any rate Lord Armond was satisfied with the service provided by Hambleden Garings. Nevertheless, Lord Armond was rather treated like royalty whenever he visited the offices or the firm entered his estate.

Lord Armond was involved with many charities and every year opened his home and grounds for a fête, charity auction and evening concert, half of the proceeds going to a well known charity and half to the upkeep of the local church.

Archie and his team conducted the charity auction, which, weather permitting, was held outside, adding to the atmosphere – reminiscent of the old market auctions of the past.

The painting that had so distressed Emilia belonged to Lord Armond, so Archie had decided to enquire at the fête whether he would indeed consider selling it privately to her.

Because of the social significance of the occasion, Mr Hambleden senior had decided that he too would attend the auction and assist Archie with lot booking, perhaps even auction a bit himself, much to Archie's concern. Mr Hambleden senior had in the past been an auctioneer of great talent and reputation, but age and a failing eyesight meant that he often received bids from the odd fly on the wall and the books didn't therefore always balance.

Mrs Hambleden, Archie's mother, was to run the cake stall. She was to sell her speciality, honey bake tarts. She also provided jars of honey to the preserves stall. Her honey was famous all over the country. People loved it. It seemed to have its own quite unique flavour.

*   *   *

On the morning of the fête, it had been tense at the office, leaving Archie and Mr Hambleden senior late for the auction. Archie had sent the staff up to Armond Hall to set things up and finally managed to drag his father away from the office and into the car.

He put his foot down and went like the wind around the winding country roads. Fortunately he could see over the tiny hedges in his four-wheel drive.

'Slow down Archie,' mumbled Mr Hambleden, 'slow down my boy.'

Archie took no notice and if anything increased his speed.

'Slow down Archie!' said a rather agitated Mr Hambleden, grabbing the handbrake and slamming it on.

The car spun, hurtled through a hole in the hedge and in pure cartoon style landed in the field at Armond Hall, not only where the fête was taking place, but near to the auctioneers' rostrum.

The whole place came to a standstill and everyone gasped as a rather shaken Mr Hambleden and a red-faced Archie got out of the Land Rover. Archie, still a little wobbly, went over to the rostrum, picked up the microphone and gavel and said, 'Right everyone, Lot 1, a pair of silver candlesticks – what's your bid?'

At the end of the fête Lord Armond announced that they had raised nearly four and a half thousand pounds and that he would match this figure to ensure both the needy causes received a suitable share. The village people applauded.

In the excitement and embarrassment of the day, Archie forgot to ask Lord Armond about the painting. When he met Emilia that evening he apologised and agreed to visit Lord Armond the next day to discuss matters, on the condition she would go out for a meal with him the following evening.

17

The next day Archie returned to Armond Hall. As he turned into the large gravel drive he saw a police car pull away and Lord Armond himself standing on the large stone steps leading to the ornate entrance.

Archie pulled up outside the door, leapt out of the car and joined Lord Armond on the steps.

'Hello sir,' he said.

'Hello my boy,' replied Lord Armond. 'How are you ?'

'I'm fine,' said Archie. 'Is everything OK, sir? Only I saw a police car driving away.'

'No dear boy, not really – come inside and I'll tell you all about it – come in and have a drink. Brandy suit?'

'Thank you sir,' said Archie, following Lord Armond into his study.

'Sit down my boy,' said Lord Armond, and explained why the police had been at the Hall.

'Last night,' he said, 'after the fête and evening concert I went to my club as usual, returned about twelve-thirty-ish and went straight to bed. About two I heard a noise and Mrs Temple, my housekeeper, came into my room, and woke me up. Apparently the old girl had gone to the bathroom and disturbed someone in

55

the dining room. I went downstairs to investigate and the blighter ran out of the French doors and up the drive. Ransacked the room – I'll show you later, but the police say we're not to touch anything, finger prints and all that. Well, I got my twelve-bore and fired it at the blighter, I think I hit him right up the derrière – just a scratch – he yelped – high pitched voice – but kept running.'

'Was anything stolen?' questioned Archie.

'Yes, it's strange really,' said Lord Armond. 'Most things were moved as though the old devil was looking for something. He left with that old painting I was going to put in the auction and then withdrew. That R.J. Langton of Lincoln cathedral – the one your father advised me to hang onto.'

'Oh,' said Archie. 'Oh dear.'

'Not the first noise Mrs Temple heard,' continued Lord Armond. 'Seems as though she heard noises in the house two or three hours before, when I was at my club. I thought she was worrying about nothing, noises in the dark and all that, but now I don't know. Sad business, but you know they didn't take the fête money or any real antiques.'

'Gosh,' said Archie, ' I don't know what to say, sir.'

'Strange business, my boy,' said Lord Armond. 'When I chased the blighter out of the French doors he didn't seem to be carrying anything, at any rate with the frame and picture how could he have run so fast? Yet the picture complete with frame is all that's gone.'

'Oh,' said Archie, not really knowing how to respond. He took another sip of his brandy and said his farewells before returning to the office.

*   *   *

Emilia dropped into the office that afternoon to arrange what time she was meeting Archie in the evening. She had been ushered into Mr Hambleden senior's room and given a coffee. Archie wouldn't be long, Lily had informed her, he was just finishing off a meeting with a client.

Ten minutes later Archie joined Emilia in Mr Hambleden's cluttered office.

'Hello,' he said. After exchanging pleasantries he relayed what had happened that morning at Armond Hall.

'Stolen?' said Emilia, sounding quite surprised. 'What, this morning?'

'Last night,' replied Archie. He didn't bore her with all the details but was struck at how surprised she was – not so much about the break-in but at the fact that something – her family painting – had gone.

'Are we still OK for this evening?' he asked, fearing that Emilia would not join him for dinner now he had not obtained the painting.

'Oh yes,' she said. 'I'm looking forward to it.'

'Good,' said Archie. 'I'll pick you up at about eight o'clock.'

'See you then,' replied Emilia. She stood up, pulling a face, and hobbled to the door.

'Are you all right?' asked Archie. 'You seem to be limping.'

'Oh,' said Emilia, 'it's nothing. I slipped this morning getting out of the bath.'

'Oh really?' said Archie. 'As long as you're all right, see you later.'

18

Archie took Emilia to a very nice restaurant near Horncastle called 'Get Stuffed'. Emilia was a bit shocked when Archie said 'Get Stuffed', thinking he no longer wanted to see her, but when they arrived at the converted stables, its sleek furnishings and lovely grounds soon impressed her. The meal was delightful and the pair got on very well.

Archie told Emilia that he had always wanted to be an auctioneer and it was assumed he would always follow in the family business. He said that there was not a day that went by that he didn't enjoy, and that it was a challenge and sometimes quite exciting.

Emilia explained that she was an art dealer and that her family had settled in the UK when she was small. Her early life had been spent overseas. She said she had a brother and talked fondly of her mother. She didn't mention her father much.

Archie didn't like to pry too much, not on a first date at any rate. He enquired as to how long Emilia would be staying in Lincolnshire and she was quite vague. She said she was researching the history of a painting and said she would stay in the area until she had completed all her enquiries.

Archie said he would help her if she wanted him to.

19

Ronald Garings sat in the drawing room of the converted chapel he shared with his wife Kitty and daughter Molly.

In about an hour his dinner guests would arrive – Archie and Emilia, Lord Armond and Mr and Mrs Soater, from number eleven. Kitty liked to invite the Soaters to all her dinners. Mr Soater was big news in finance and property, she would say, keen for Ronald to progress his career. She had long thought his partnership in Hambleden Garings was more a status title and a way of Archie getting his hands on some of the Garings' fortune rather than an equal partnership.

Ronald was the only son of Mr and Mrs Albert Garings. He had come from a modest background, but his father, a rather astute man, bought up several shoe shops in the 1960s and was able to sell them for a handsome profit, some being in prime town and city redevelopment zones. The sales allowed the Garings to enjoy a comfortable retirement and Ronald and his younger sister Martha to pursue their chosen careers: Ronald in estate agency and Martha in the tourism industry.

Ronald's mother was a sweet old lady who had always helped his father in the shops, but in later life had become very involved with local charities. Ronald was thinking about this when a broad smile came over his face. He remembered how, one particular day when he and Kitty were staying at his parents' home while the chapel was being converted, his mother had reminded him that Archie's mother had organised some jumble for him to collect at the office for her local church fête.

'Yes mother, I'll remember to get the jumble,' Ronald had said.

Later that day Ronald had returned to his car to find a bin bag of clothes on the back seat. So that night he dutifully took it home for his mother's fête, only to discover that the bag of clothes was in fact Archie's freshly washed laundry, done by Mrs Hambleden and returned to the wrong car by Mr Hambleden senior.

'Easy mistake,' Kitty had said. 'Archie's clothes would well suit a jumble sale.'

*　　*　　*

Kitty had hurried round all day making the house tidy, ensuring the food was prepared to perfection and the wine chilled. She liked to make a good impression – after all Archie was Ronald's business partner (although in her opinion he rather took her husband for granted). Lord Armond was a delight and the Soaters were a lovely couple.

Archie was to bring the mysterious Emilia Langton, who appeared from nowhere at one of the auctions and ever since that mix-up over the painting which had been stolen at Armond Hall appeared to be a regular companion of Archie's. Kitty was rather looking forward to meeting her – she needed to find out how serious she was about Archie; after all the partnership could be affected.

*　　*　　*

On the way to Ronald and Kitty's house, Emilia sat very quietly in the passenger seat of Archie's Land Rover.

'You're quiet,' said Archie. 'All right?'

'Yes, I'm fine,' she replied, thinking about the fiasco with the painting. Emilia was indeed R.J. Langton's great-great-granddaughter and it was this fact that had encouraged her to take an interest in paintings, antiques and jewellery in her youth. She had combined this interest with her job in the police force.

She was, in actual fact, a detective, assigned to investigate the whereabouts of several missing paintings and trinkets that had been stolen from galleries, museums and private collections and smuggled out of the country by clever bidding and transferring through auction lots. The Hambleden Garings auction house seemed to be a possible route of trade, being suitably located close to the Lincolnshire coast and Humberside airport.

Emilia had befriended the hapless Archie with a view to gaining an insight into the auction system and keeping an eye on lots bought and sold. More importantly, it allowed her to become familiar with the identities of the sellers and buyers.

She felt sure that something strange had been going on with the R.J. Langton painting. She had closely followed its progress of sale from a London auction house, to a Scottish house, back to London, then to Norfolk, before returning to Lincolnshire. She had originally watched its progress because the painting had been one of her great-great grandfather's, but soon realised it was attracting a lot of interest. Yes it was lovely, but it hadn't been done by one of the country's great masters.

Interestingly, a favourite lot number for the smugglers was suspected to be twenty-two. Although not fully proven, Emilia's research seemed to suggest this and the R.J. Langton painting seemed to be linked many times with this lot number.

When Archie had failed to obtain the painting for her from

Lord Armond, she felt she ought to find out more about it herself. Why had it been withdrawn from the sale? She was sadly disturbed by Lord Armond's housekeeper, Mrs Temple, and only by the skin of her teeth escaped Armond Hall and Lord Armond's gunshots with a scratched and rather sore backside. She was however puzzled that the painting had gone missing and that the thief – so everyone had thought – was the intruder on fête night – in other words, her. But Emilia didn't want to steal it, just examine it for clues, and she certainly hadn't taken it. Someone must have got there before her – but who? Or was Lord Armond hiding something himself? If so, why did he put the painting in the auction and withdraw it so quickly? Why would he want to draw attention to it if he was in fact part of the smuggling ring?

* * *

When the guests arrived at the Garings, they sat round the dinner table discussing every subject from the weather to holidays, politics, art and of course Lord Armond's break-in and the possible whereabouts of the missing painting.

'What made you decide to sell it and then withdraw it from the sale, sir?' asked Emilia.

'Advice of a friend,' replied Lord Armond. 'It was suggested that in time it could prove to be a lucrative investment – but who knows? Indeed, who knows if I will ever see it again?'

A lucrative investment, thought Emilia, I wonder what he means? It's lovely but not that good an investment when compared to some of the old masters. She was about to ask him some more questions when Kitty suggested they change the subject.

'Lord Armond doesn't want bothering with his problems when he's dining with friends. He should be allowed to relax and forget things for an hour or two,' she said.

To break the tension between Kitty and Emilia, Ronald suggested they all try some of Mrs Hambleden's honey rum, which Archie had bought with him as a gift to the hosting couple. Everyone enjoyed this liqueur, which was consumed through a blob of fresh cream.

'Unusual combination, made presumably from the honey from Mrs Hambleden's famous bees,' said Lord Armond.

'No,' replied Archie. 'The honey comes from the trees.'

Everyone stared, but by now were too relaxed to question him further.

* * *

'You were quiet and didn't eat a lot this evening,' said Archie to Emilia, when they were driving home. 'Everything all right?'

'Yes,' said Emilia, 'I'm fine, I was just tired.'

'You should have had some of Mother's honey rum, that would have relaxed you.'

'Well, I promised you I would drive,' said Emilia, 'and I won't drink and drive.'

'Good idea, good idea indeed, because if you and I, being me being I had drunk then we would have . . . erm, had to walk and it's cold and I would have had to walk.' Archie burped and giggled like a schoolboy.

'Oh God, Archie, how much did you drink?' asked Emilia. She was tired, cold and hungry. She hadn't eaten much at the Garings, because she had to pretend she had a small appetite so as not to offend Kitty. Kitty had gone to a lot of trouble with the meal, but she had done turkey and all the trimmings for the main course. Emilia could eat most things, she would try most dishes, but she hated turkey, she couldn't bear the smell. She daren't say anything to Kitty though. She already sensed Kitty was wary of her. She didn't want to cause any upset. Also she would have liked to have talked more about the painting with Lord Armond, but Kitty was having none of it. And now she had a middle-aged man in the car pissed as newt and behaving like a silly schoolboy.

Emilia drove Archie's Land Rover through what appeared to be thick fog.

'This isn't fog,' said Emilia. 'I can smell petrol fumes, I think we're travelling through smoke not fog. Someone might be in trouble.'

'Oooh, I think I am,' said Archie, winding the window down. 'I think I'm going to be sick.'

As Archie wound the window down, he and Emilia passed a white rusty Metro parked up on the side of the road. Its engine was still running and smoke was pouring out of the back. Two women stood by the side of the car, and they waved at Archie and Emilia, asking them to stop.

Emilia wound her window down. 'Are you all right?'

'No,' said one woman, 'our car has broken down.' They noticed Archie in the passenger seat with his head hung out of the window.

'Hi Archie,' they said, 'all right there, boss?'

'Oh, hello ladies,' replied Archie, 'what are you busy about? Look Emilia, it's Trish Medler and Julie Armstrong from our Louth office.'

'The car's broken down, Archie, we're stranded,' said Trish. 'Can we have a lift?'

'Of course,' said Archie, 'no problem, no problem at all. If I was you ladies I would get a new car, always thought that was a pile of crap.'

'It's a company car,' said Julie. 'Trish and I have been on a course for work and the car's been running strange all day, we thought we might just make it home, but . . .'

64

'A company car? Oh yes,' said Archie and giggled. 'I suppose as I'm your boss then, it's my problem, not yours.'

Archie staggered out of the Land Rover. 'Give me the keys,' he said.

He undid the boot of the Metro and took a Hambleden Garings For Sale board out and put it in the front window.

'Right girlies, get in the back of the Land Rover, Emilia is taking us all home and you never know, we might just be able to sell that rust-bucket. Get Ronald to do some marketing particulars on it in the morning, let's get the bloody thing sold.'

Archie then passed out.

* * *

Archie had some serious making up to do with Emilia the next day. She was really upset and agitated by his drunken behaviour. He wasn't a drinker really but he did like his mother's honey rum. Nursing a sore head he apologised to Emilia with flowers and chocolates. She didn't want to know at first, so he stood in her hotel car park singing at the top of his voice so all could hear. He couldn't sing, but the guitar player, drummer and backing track he had hired sounded pretty good and drowned out his singing a bit. After three verses of Archie and co singing 'I Just Called to Say I Love You', a red-faced but secretly rather chuffed Emilia joined him in the car park. All was forgiven.

20

An extra buzz of excitement filled the Hewton and Terry offices
the following Monday. Vernon was strutting about ordering
everyone to their places. All the staff were at work, full- and part-
time. All uniforms had been cleaned and shoes polished, even
the cleaner had arrived in her suit, the one she had worn for her
daughter's wedding the month before.

The popular *House Hunter* programme was visiting the area to
do a home search for a member of the public. 'A *House Hunter*
special, concentrating on rural properties,' Vernon had announced
to his staff. 'One of our properties has been chosen, a converted
barn close to the coast.'

The only snag had been that the barn was unfurnished and
to qualify for the programme all properties had to be furnished.
Vernon's client lived abroad and gave him permission to go ahead
with allowing the house to be featured on TV and, at his own
expense, Vernon was going to furnish it.

'A few bits and pieces from home,' he told his wife, Rebecca.
'And the rest,' she thought.

* * *

66

Vernon was in his fifties and on his second marriage. He had had four daughters with his first wife; three worked in the estate agency and one was at university. He had a seven-year-old son with Rebecca, who was some twenty years his junior. Rebecca was a fierce woman who had caused the end of his first marriage. She even pursued Vernon and his first wife Isobel while they were on holiday in Umbria, trying to repair their marriage following his initial affair with Rebecca being discovered by Isobel.

Vernon had kept Isobel short of money when they were married and it was a struggle for her to obtain funds from him to support her and the children after their separation. She got her revenge though, by publishing her story in a gossip magazine, ensuring her picture looked much better than Rebecca's. The magazine sold out in the town within hours.

Vernon somehow seemed to like the fame and kept a copy of the article in his private papers at the office. The article did say that Vernon was a handsome chap – the most likely reason why he had hung onto the article.

Vernon and Isobel's relationship had improved over the years and financially he had started to provide for and help his family. Much to the distaste of Rebecca.

* * *

A TV feature would be an excellent advertisement for his firm. It would also wipe the smile off that Archie Hambleden's face.

The TV company making *House Hunter* were to do a brief interview with Vernon at his office and then look at the converted barn.

Due to the tight filming schedule the piece would be filmed that Monday and shown on TV on the Thursday evening. 'More realistic, more true to life,' said the director. Things had gone very well, Vernon thought, when the camera team left the office. He had been quite authoritative on the housing market in the area.

The furnishings in the barn were superb and the staff looked happy and smart. Even his father, a retired farmer and viewing consultant, didn't try to take over the limelight. 'Too busy keeping a low profile after showing a couple round the wrong house the other Saturday, I shouldn't wonder,' thought Vernon. Silly fool; the arrangement was to collect the key for the house under the pot outside 27 Holly Road, not 17. Oh, there was a key but the occupiers of the house didn't expect Pops Hewton to come charging in wearing his hand-knitted jumper, lovingly made by his wife with 'POPS' emblazoned across the chest, with a load of viewers – not while they were having their breakfast and still in their night gear, particularly as their home was not for sale.

* * *

'Come on Archie,' said Emilia, 'we should watch *House Hunter*, normally you like the show.'

'I know,' said Archie 'but that idiot Vermin will be on it. What he knows about property you could write on a postage stamp. Although I must admit I have set the video, thought I might pluck up the courage to watch it later.'

'Oh, don't be silly,' teased Emilia. 'Watch it now, I'd like to see it.' So Archie and Emilia settled down to watch *House Hunter*.

First the presenter talked about the area, then she conducted a brief interview about the property market with Vernon.

'All teeth and slime,' mumbled Archie. 'Sitting there in his Armani suit, on the knock I shouldn't wonder.'

'Archie Hambleden,' said Emilia, 'I do believe you're jealous.'

'No I'm not,' said Archie, and started to laugh. 'Well maybe a little. He's a horrible man though, you know. He's destroyed many a career in his time. Will stop at nothing to be top dog, devious cocky, nasty self-preserving, twisting shit – a thief, a thief in every sense of the word.'

'Nice guy then,' replied Emilia.

The cameras moved to the barn conversion.

'He furnished that himself,' said Archie. 'Must have set him back a bit, probably nicked the money from some unsuspecting ex-business partner or client. That one lives by the sword and will die by the sword.'

'Shut up a minute, Archie,' shouted Emilia. 'Did you say the video was on?'

'Yes,' said Archie. 'I could switch it off as I'm watching this idiot now.'

'No don't do that, keep it recording,' said Emilia.

The pair watched the video replay and because it was new, state of the art, quite daring for Archie, they were able to zoom in close on items of interest.

'Look,' said Emilia.

'A painting of Picasso's *Dora Maar Au Chat*,' replied Archie. 'I shouldn't worry, it's likely to be a poster or print, like the one on auction day which replaced your great-great-grandfather's painting. Vernon's favourite painter is Picasso. In fact it pains me to admit he's quite knowledgeable about the painter. Still, I doubt even he's able to afford an original, particularly not that one. The original has recently been bought by a mystery collector at auction for a significant sum of money; I believe it was bought for over 95 million US dollars, making it the second-highest price ever paid for a painting at auction.'

'No, no,' said Emilia, 'look at the frame – it's the same as the R.J. Langton frame.'

'Well there are hundreds of frames like that.'

'There's a mark on the frame in the corner, see?' said Emilia, zooming the video in further.

'Difficult to tell,' said Archie 'the pause still does rather distort things.'

'We need to see the frame close up,' said Emilia. 'My great-great-grandfather always used to sign his painting and initial the frame. A little gimmick which he hoped one day might engage the purchasing public.'

'Now Emilia,' said Archie, 'how can we get into the property and look? I'm really going to say to Vermin, "let's look at the barn, I think there's a mark on the frame on that painting in the lounge". Besides which , it maybe a different R.J. Langton frame.'

'Archie, we need to get into the barn and have a look at that frame,' interrupted Emilia. 'Each initial was in a slightly different place on the frames, so each of my grandfather's frames was unique. Plus I marked it with a pen at the viewing day so I knew what to bid for.'

'But Vernon put all the furniture in the property,' said Archie. 'What are you suggesting?'

'I don't know,' said Emilia. 'All I know is we need to get to that barn and examine that frame.'

After dark Archie and Emilia drove to the barn. They were certain no one saw them as it was quite isolated. 'If we're spotted,' said Emilia, 'we simply say we're part of the TV crew tidying up.'

'Uh,' Archie grumbled, 'everyone knows me, it's all right for you.'

Archie was amazed at how easily Emilia was able to pick the lock of the back door.

'All those years at university paid off,' she said, turning and winking at Archie as she pushed the door open.

Archie consoled himself by the fact that the electricity was switched off, so at least there would be no alarm.

The pair went straight to the lounge. All the furniture was still in place but the Picasso print and frame had gone. Archie saw a piece of paper on the floor, on the back of which was written, 'VENICE'.

21

The next morning the Hambleden Garings staff met for their regular breakfast meeting. It had been Ronald's idea – trendy big city firms always had breakfast meetings. Only a trendy breakfast meeting at Hambleden Garings consisted of a cup of tea or coffee and a round of toast and butter if you were lucky. Very high-powered. One morning Sidney had served up a spoonful of ants in Ronald's tea; he claimed he hadn't seen them happily nesting in the sugar bowl. A likely story, but nevertheless it did brighten the meeting up somewhat.

Archie was late for the meeting this particular morning.

'Well if he doesn't arrive soon,' said Ronald, 'I'll start without him.'

'Oh, he'll be here soon,' said Belinda, the weekend and holiday cover agent.

'Good,' said Adrian Kingston, the financial adviser. 'I'm starving, I'm ready for my breakfast. My wife has had me on this strict diet for ages, lettuce leaves, tomatoes and fibre stuff, also this funny cake bar thing. Supposed to make you feel as though you've eaten a three course meal, all in this funny cake bar thing. The adverts say it's a tasty treat, it looks like cake, it tastes fantastic, it's a meal in a bar. It should say it looks like shit, it tastes like shit, in fact, it is shit. God, why is dieting so boring? If I could invent chocolate-flavoured lettuce I'd make a fortune, an absolute fortune, dreamt about chocolate last night, it was . . .'

'Shut up going on,' said Belinda. 'Anyway, how much have you lost?'

'Well nothing,' replied Adrian, tucking into a Mars Bar he produced from his jacket pocket.

'My wife thinks I should see a doctor to ensure that there's nothing wrong with me.'

Everyone stared at him in amazement, but before they could comment that perhaps his frequent snacks might be the cause of his lack of weight loss, Archie arrived.

'Sorry to keep you waiting,' he said, 'I've been trying to get hold of Vernon Hewton, but his mobile is off and the staff at his office haven't turned up yet – typical late starters, not like us of course.'

'Why do you want to speak to Vernon?' asked an insecure Ronald.

'Market business,' snapped Archie. He actually wanted to talk to Vernon about the events of the past few days.

'Oh, he's gone to Venice for a few days on business, my sister sorted out the tickets,' said Ronald.

After the morning meeting, Archie rang Emilia. 'How do you fancy a trip to Venice?' he asked.

22

Vernon had gone on his trip to Venice without his wife, and Archie was determined to get to the bottom of things relating to the mystery of the painting of the cathedral by R.J. Langton and the Picasso print with the R.J. Langton frame.

Emilia was happy to accept Archie's invitation to Venice – the mystery of the missing painting was the only lead she had in her investigations. Was the slimy Vernon Hewton something to do with the smuggling? She should investigate all areas. She needed something positive. Success with this case could mean promotion.

'Venice is full of canals and narrow streets,' said Emilia to Archie. 'It provides a good hiding place for antiques and the antiques trade; I wonder what Vernon is up to, if anything?'

'Oh, he's up to something,' said Archie. 'You can be sure of that.'

'You really like him don't you?' laughed Emilia.

'Terrific fellow,' said Archie, smiling.

Emilia sat on the plane reading her pocket guide about the city. It said: '*Any visitor to Venice has to confront its unique geography. To explore the city properly you have to be prepared to pound the streets – in fact this is a pleasure in such a car-free environment – and to cross the many bridges that span the canals. When walking becomes tiring, take to the water aboard the vapretto (water bus). The main vapretto routes are on the Grand Canal, but the system will also take you out to the far corners of the lagoon, from the beaches at the lido and the brightly painted houses of the Island of Burano to the wall to wall glass showrooms and factories on Murano and the medieval cathedral set amid the salt meadows on the Island of Torcello'.*

Emilia and Archie checked into their hotel, which was centrally located just off St Mark's Square. It was a well maintained establishment, and provided the ideal base for following Vernon, who was staying close by, also just off St Mark's Square.

'He must not know we're here,' said Archie.

'He doesn't,' replied Emilia. 'We'll keep an eye on what he's doing, we can blend in with the tourists.' Emilia was confident in her detective skills, but she couldn't blame Archie for his concerns – after all, he didn't know her background.

Archie knew his way around Venice quite well and had many business contacts in the city, but couldn't help but worry that he and Emilia would be noticed by Vernon if they were not careful. It's one thing tailing someone on your own, but when there are two of you it's much harder. Perhaps he shouldn't have asked Emilia to join him after all. But on the other hand, two brains are better than one.

* * *

The next day, suitably rested, Emilia and Archie set about tailing Vernon round the historic narrow streets and waterways of Venice.

'There was disastrous flooding in Venice in 1966, local and international organisations were set up to restore buildings in the city and bring Venice's plight to national attention. The industrial area of Porto Marghera takes millions of gallons of lagoon water, which has added to the problems. There are plans in place, future and ongoing, to improve the situation, however, the Italian bureaucratic system, which is quite notorious for being slow and difficult, has hindered the speed of the improvements. There is an increasing problem in winter with high water flooding.' Archie tried to remember his degree studies on the History of Art and Architecture word for word. He said all this because he was trying to impress Emilia with his extensive knowledge of the City. He went on to say, 'In fact, the rhythm of Venice is like music, high water, fast, loud music, intense. Low water, relaxed soothing, gentle music, softly in the background. This is often featured in the performance of St Mark's Square's various orchestras which play daily.'

Archie stood admiring the architecture, and then began to walk backwards to take in the full view of the buildings he loved so much.

'Just look at that,' he said, 'Just look at . . .'

He fell backwards into the canal, much to the amusement of onlookers.

'Archie?! ARCHIE! Are you all right?' shouted a concerned Emilia.

'Yes, YES!' snapped Archie, splashing and spluttering.

One of the local gondoliers had to lasso him in the water and pull him to the safety of his gondola. There was a party of sightseeing holidaymakers sat in it, all trying not to laugh. Archie felt quite embarrassed, not to mention wet. His mood was not helped by the laughter of the holidaymakers and Emilia, who up until then had let Archie show off his obvious knowledge of the city, even though secretly she knew it like the back of her hand. After Archie's fall however, she could no longer hold back her amusement and burst out laughing. Between giggles she couldn't resist asking him what rhythm of music he was feeling after his fall.

Irritated, Archie retreated back to the hotel, leaving Emilia to tail Vernon on her own.

*   *   *

Vernon went to an antique shop near St Mark's cathedral. He then went to the Museo Correr (the local museum of art and jewellery). He was carrying a rolled up tube. He left the museum and went to another antiques shop and gallery. He left minus the tube but now he was carrying a Puma sports bag. He then bought some Venetian chocolates and biscuits and went straight onto the *vapretto*, back to the airport.

Interesting, thought Emilia. Very few changes of clothes – clearly not a social visit. What was in that tube? What was in the sports bag? She made some notes for her superiors in the police force.

*   *   *

Vernon was very very pleased with himself. He had made a very good deal here in wonderful Venice with his city contact, Henry Stanley, who was based at the Museo Correr. Perhaps he could soon now install a swimming pool at his house. That should keep his wife happy.

Yes, it had been quite a few weeks really, everything seemed to be going his way right now. A good TV appearance, a successful firm and now a successful business trip to Venice.

He would return to this amazing city in a couple of weeks.

He sat back in his plane seat with a self-satisfied grin on his face and his hand firmly holding the Puma bag he had picked up in Venice.

23

Back at Hambleden Garings things had been quite normal really.
Mr Hambleden senior was running things in his own unique way.
He had decided to take the two trainees with him to a house
inspection. In the car, as usual, he had his head turned round
facing them, testing them on their times tables. He was so busy
with this he forgot that he was driving and drove straight up the
planks forming a ramp into the back of an empty removal van.
The trainees shouted in disbelief and distress.

Even his beloved satnav was confused. 'You have taken the
wrong turning,' it repeated, seemingly in distress.

Mr Hambleden slammed on the breaks of his Rover car just
in time before hitting the end wall of the removal truck. He didn't
say a word, just reversed as though nothing had happened.

At this stage the removal men were returning to the van. All
they could do was stare at Mr Hambleden's Rover as it reversed
and pulled away.

Later Mr Hambleden was covered in moisture from a crop
sprayer. He hadn't realised it was situated behind a hedge as he
left his car to commence an agricultural inventory.

The final straw was when he parked on double yellow lines
outside the office – just for five minutes while he collected his

newspaper. A lady jumped into the back of the car believing he was a taxi – she thought the satnav screen was the meter. Together with her shopping and snappy dog, she filled the car and took some shifting.

* * *

On his return from Venice, Archie asked his father whether anything out of the ordinary had happened while he had been away.

'No,' was his reply, 'just an ordinary day.'

'Good,' said Archie.

'Everything all right with you and Emilia?' asked Mr Hambleden.

'Yes,' said Archie, sneezing – feeling the effects of his fall into the canal. 'Don't worry, everything went very well – all sorted, it's fine, just fine.'

'Good,' replied Mr Hambleden. 'Business as usual then my boy.'

'For the time being, Father, yes I think so,' replied Archie.

'Good, good. Where's Emilia?'

'Oh she'll be back in a day or two, Father, she's staying in London, visiting family.'

* * *

Mrs Benita Hambleden had attended her weekly line dancing class with the Richmond County Liners at Skegness. They were a mixed bag of dancers, some quite brilliant, some not so brilliant, some who thought they were brilliant, but weren't really.

Mrs Hambleden was a fairly average dancer, but she enjoyed the evening, as Mr Hambleden didn't like dancing and at any

79

rate found it difficult with his walking stick. It was a place she could go with her friends, a place she was able to go without him and his flipping satnav, which he seemed to carry round with him ever since the staff bought it for him as one of his many leaving presents.

'Look,' said Hazel Jacklin, one of Benita's dancing friends. 'The new dancer on the front row; is that Rebecca Hewton? You know, the estate agent's wife? His name's Vernon I think. Do you know him? I don't, but that Rebecca I know her, she's come from the gutter you know, the gutter, but now look at her. She does think herself somebody, stuck-up cow. Do you know she was collecting for charity once and said to me, if I couldn't afford the collection I didn't have to donate. Who does she think she is? My Frank could buy her and her husband out three times over.'

'Oh yes,' said Benita, 'I know Vernon Hewton all right.' Benita said very little else, just cringed at the name Vernon – the very thought of the man made her feel sick.

Hazel made her way to the bar. 'Another drink, Benita?' she asked.

'Make it a double,' said Benita.

A young barman came over to serve Hazel. 'Did you used to work in Wilko's?' she enquired, smiling at him intently.

'No,' he replied, 'the wine bar up the road – madam, are you chatting me up?'

'Young man,' said Hazel, 'I'd love to chat you up, really love to, but I'm way too old for you.'

He just laughed.

'Honestly,' said Benita, 'pull yourself together, Hazel, he's less than half your age at least.'

'Well, you can't blame a girl for trying,' smiled Hazel.

'What about your Frank? said Benita. 'And "a girl"! If you were an estate agent you do realise you would be done for misdescription. Anyway have you told your Frank yet you're going to retire?'

'Yes,' said Hazel looking glum. 'He just said he couldn't understand why I should want to retire as I wear a nice suit for work, silly fool him, bugger the fact that I want some quality time at home for myself, he wants me to keep working because our office uniform is nice. Honestly.'

Benita just laughed.

*　　*　　*

Back in Venice, things were far from normal for Italian-born Henry Stanley. He had just had a useful business meeting with Vernon Hewton. A meeting which might change things for him, his family and his friends. He had had many adventures over the years, some good some not so good. But now at least he was happy. He had a good job in Venice and a loving family. He smiled as he sat at his desk, remembering when he first visited Venice and met his wife, Dutch-born Monica and her family, who had moved from Holland some years earlier. Monica was an expert in diamonds. Henry's mother-in-law always called her husband *Lieveling*, which is Dutch for 'darling'. Henry didn't realise this and when introduced to Monica's father started calling him *Lieveling*, thinking it was his name, which much amused Monica and her family. It was a long while before they told him the real meaning of *Lieveling*.

Henry's wife's family were very supportive of him and offered him the stability and love he needed after his traumatic start in life. He was still haunted by his past and hoped that his meeting with Vernon would put that right and soon he and his family could start afresh.

24

Two Weeks Later

Vernon could not help feeling pleased with himself. Since the TV programme, *House Hunter*, he had been fortunate enough to travel all over the world. His new-found fame seemed to open many doors, helping his ultimate mission. All-expenses-paid trips to some of the loveliest cities in the world: New York, Paris, Rome, Bruges and his personal favourite, the floating city, Venice.

His wife was not impressed she had to stay at home and look after young Vernon. This was the second time in the matter of weeks Vernon was returning to Venice without her.

But never mind, expensive gifts and the lure of a cruise later in the year had smoothed things over. 'Business after all,' he thought, 'should be separate from family holidays.' Still, as he sat on the *vapretto* about to dock near St Mark's Square, he felt a slight pang of guilt – perhaps he should have brought Rebecca with him this time. But then she would have to be told his secret and, although they were married, he was not sure he could really trust her.

Vernon had fallen under the spell of Venice. A vast and beautiful city of red roofs, bells and towers drifting across the lagoon like a large boat in a haze of mist. Crumbling stone and brick and the odd stolen glimpse in the apartments facing the lagoon as the *vapretto* passed by indicated the wealth of the city. Chandeliers, gold-embossed handles and mosaic-covered ceilings and walls were frequently on display.

Vernon checked into his hotel, the Bauer Palace, an ornately furnished property, originally a large town house, likely to have been the home of a merchant, close to St Mark's Square and with its own water taxi landing spot to the rear.

Vernon lay on his hotel bed feeling a bit seasick after his water bus trip. He heard a noise near the door; a note had been passed under it. It said: '*Welcome to Venice, Basilica St Marco, 11:30. Near four horses*'.

Vernon checked his watch. It was eleven o'clock, which gave him half an hour to get washed and changed and navigate his way to St Mark's Basilica through the hundreds of tourists and pigeons.

Vernon entered the Basilica, and made his way over the magnificent marble floor embellished with twelfth-century mosaics showing figures of animals alternating with geometrical patterns. He looked in awe at the mosaics, which resembled an enormous illustrated Bible.

In 1204, Venetian crusaders decided to conquer Constantinople. After a sturdy defence by the Greeks the city was taken, and many treasures were transported to Venice, including four bronze horses which now rest in St Mark's Basilica. There were replicas of the horses on the external wall facing the square, but Vernon knew his meeting was going to be near the originals, which were roped off but visible to the public inside the magnificent building.

A tall, slim man with dark hair and a wiry moustache stood near the horses reading the information cards about their history.

Vernon stood next to him and said 'What wonderful statues, it's quite amazing how the light seems to dance in their eyes.'

'Quite ingenious,' replied the man. 'Mr Vernon I assume? Henry Stanley described you to me.'

He handed a sports bag to Vernon and told him to open it in private. 'Details will accompany the object,' he said.

He then left. Vernon waited five minutes and then left also. He was excited about this meeting at St Mark's. He left the Basilica quarter and couldn't wait to get back to his hotel room to examine the contents of the bag.

He strode across St Mark's Square, packed with ornate buildings. The various orchestras were playing, and tourists had gathered to watch them. Vernon found his strides change in time with the music, and he almost skipped back to his room, dodging the puddles of water on the Square's flagstones caused by the high tide of the lagoon. He was so excited that at last he was getting somewhere. The orchestras were playing Vivaldi's *Four Seasons*, and Vernon could not help humming as he skipped and walked, his heart beating in time with the music like a big bass drum. The music reached its moving finish, just as Vernon arrived back at his hotel. He was in too much of a hurry to wait for the lift so took the marble-tiled stairs two at a time. He rushed along the ornately decorated landing, which displayed many Canelletto prints. Vernon had no time to admire them, and in his haste took three attempts to activate the key card from red to green.

His room had been tidied, his window had been left open and the silk curtains, partially drawn, danced in the gentle breeze. Vernon opened the sports bag. Inside was a cardboard box containing a black pottery cat. Nice touch he thought. He took hold of the cat and smashed its head against the tiled floor. The ornament broke into tiny pieces, revealing the equivalent in euro notes to ten thousand pounds, a list of details, directions and dates, together with an invitation which said:

Auction 20 May: Automobilia sale at 3 p.m., motor car sale at 5p.m. Les Grandes Marques a Monaco on sale at Musée Automobile de la Collection de SAS le Prince de Monaco. INVITATION.

Vernon had an invitation to attend one of the most important European auctions of sports, competition and collectors' motor cars and related automobilia. There was also a page from the sale catalogue – Lot 22 was circled – a green 35B-type Bugatti C8.

Vernon felt both excited and nervous – he knew what he had to do.

* * *

Vernon hired a gondola so he could take in some of the wonderful sights of Venice and admire them from the canals – the only way really to appreciate this unique city. Nothing is more Venetian than the gondola. Gondolas have existed since the eleventh century, and today there are about 500 in the city. All gondolas are made to the same specification, built by hand from barely three hundred pieces of wood. The left side of the gondola is wider than the right. Many gondoliers still wear the traditional outfit of straw boater, striped T-shirt and white sailor's top, although these days, if you want to be serenaded, that will cost extra.

Vernon's gondola travelled along the canal near to the Rialto Bridge, wonderful! His mind wandered to a time that seemed so long ago. Thirty years or so had passed since he lived in Italy. What a wonderful experience it had been, quite liberating, the making of him.

His calm was interrupted quite abruptly. A gun shot sounded and what felt like a bullet just missed him. It whistled past his ear. The gondolier ducked and then asked Vernon if he was all right.

'Yes,' he snapped, 'just get me back to my hotel.'

Vernon was shaken up. He convinced himself it was an accident, youths messing with an air rifle that got out of hand or something. He refused to believe the bullet was meant for him. He certainly wasn't going to report the incident – how paranoid people would think he was?

*　*　*

She shot the gun, but changed her mind when it was too late. God, had she killed him? Thank God he was still alive, she had missed. She always was a poor shot. She pushed the gun into her bag so that no one would realise it was her and ran off the Rialto Bridge crying. Damn him, damn that rotten man, she would find him, she would kill him, but not like this, not today.

She was joined by a younger man at the end of the Rialto, puffing from his run after her. He gave her a hug.

'This is not the way,' he said. 'We will sort him, but not like this.'

'Promise?' she said.

'I promise,' he replied. 'Come on, let's get you home.'

25

It was Rebecca's birthday, and Vernon held a massive party at their trendy home for her. He invited all their friends, plus contacts and business colleagues. Archie and Emilia were invited along with Mr and Mrs Hambleden. It was a lavish do – no expense was spared.

Archie and Emilia arrived fashionably late, and the party was in full flow.

'Nibbles and champagne, naff music and false kindness,' muttered Archie.

'Oh come on grumpy – you may enjoy it,' said Emilia. 'Look, let's go and join your parents.'

'That bloody Vernon is a show-off,' said Mrs Hambleden. 'Slimy irritating big head.'

'I can see you get your cheerfulness and fondness for Vernon from Archie,' laughed Emilia.

Halfway through the evening Vernon stood on the central staircase in his open lounge/diner and called for quiet. The orchestra he had hired stopped playing.

'I just want to say a few words,' he said. 'As you know it's my darling Rebecca's birthday.'

Everyone clapped. Rebecca smiled.

'I just want to wish her all the best and give her her present,' said Vernon. 'Please come and join me here, Rebecca.'

Rebecca joined Vernon on the bottom step of the stairs. Two Hewton and Terry staff members walked forward carrying a large object covered in a cloth. Everyone clapped as Rebecca pulled away the cloth. It revealed a Picasso print of *Dora Maar Au Chat*.

'Signed by the artist,' shouted Vernon so all could hear.

'God,' said Emilia to Archie. 'It's the painting – it's in the R.J. Langton frame.'

'Bloody hell,' said Archie. 'It's signed – I think you're right, it's the frame.'

'We need to examine it,' said Emilia.

'I agree,' said Archie, 'but not now, not here.'

* * *

The next day Archie and Emilia waited outside Vernon's house in a rented truck – so they would not be recognised. Vernon left for work as usual and Rebecca left the house about an hour later to take young Vernon to school. Satisfied that the house was empty, Archie and Emilia drove to the front door. Again Emilia amazed Archie at how quickly she could break into a property. She took the ladder left in the open-fronted garage, propped it up on the wall and pushed open the already slightly open sash window to the rear of the house. She ran downstairs, deactivated the alarm and let Archie in the front door.

'How did you know the code?' asked Archie.

'I checked last night – codes written on the side of the alarm case – you'd be surprised at how many people leave their alarm codes on view. The upper window there is always slightly open – I've noticed it before – some people are so trusting! And I moved the ladder yesterday evening when I went to powder my nose.'

'You're very observant and resourceful. Don't tell me – they taught you to be observant and resourceful at university.'

The pair searched the house, and found the print in the study, waiting to be hung on the wall. Archie lifted it onto a chair so they could examine it more easily and in his usual clumsy fashion accidentally knocked it off the chair onto the floor. The glass smashed and the print fell out as he and Emilia lifted it back onto the chair.

'Oh God, Archie – you idiot – you clumsy idiot!' yelled Emilia.

'Emilia, look!' said Archie, looking pale.

A brown envelope had fallen from the back of the print. Emilia opened it.

'It's . . . Jesus!' said Emilia, hardly able to speak. 'It's documents of authenticity for the Doge's Diamonds.'

'The Doge's Diamonds?' said Archie. 'Do they really exist?'

'Well it looks like they do,' said Emilia, 'and according to this they're hidden in Monaco.'

'Are they fake documents or the real thing?' questioned Archie.

'I studied them at university,' said Emilia. 'They look very genuine to me, but I thought they were in a private collection in Venice. God, do you think Vernon stole these when he went to Venice?'

* * *

Rebecca arrived home and was surprised to see a truck on the drive. She looked across the garden and saw Mr Antony, her gardener. 'He usually comes on his bike,' she thought, 'didn't realise he had a truck and could drive.' She opened the front door of the house and went to put the kettle on. She wasn't keen on the gardener having a key to her house and knowing the alarm code, but Vernon certainly wasn't going to waste his spare time gardening, so what could she do?

* * *

'Shush,' whispered Emilia, 'I can hear someone.'

Archie peered out of the window. 'Rebecca's back,' he said.

'Damn!' said Emilia 'What now?'

Archie noticed the keys to the French doors sat in the lock. He unlocked them and they crept out onto the patio 'I didn't need to go to university to realise people leave door keys in locks all the time,' he smirked.

'Shush,' said Emilia, 'Rebecca will hear us if we're not careful.'

The pair climbed over the decorative patio terrace wall into the side garden. Mr Antony had parked his ride-on mower near this area while he went into the greenhouse. He noticed the pair leaving the house. He ran out of the greenhouse shouting at them as he did so.

'Oi! What you up to?' he gasped.

Archie and Emilia jumped onto the ride-on mower. Archie pulled the starter and the pair sped off round the lawn and through a gap in the hedge. Mr Antony ran after them, but soon had to stop to catch his breath. The mower hurtled down the hill by Vernon's house. The vibration of the potholes on the road loosened the frame, which was detachable from the engine and steering wheel for ease of transportation. With a clonk the mower engine and steering part went into the hedge, leaving Emilia and Archie on the back frame, belting down the hill with no means of braking.

'Oh God, Archhhiee, whattt aaare weee ggoing tttoooo dooo?' screamed Emilia over the vibration of the mower frame.

'SMMMmmile,' he replied. 'Wee are about tooooo enter the Belchford Dow ..., Downhill Challenge.'

Every year competitors enter a downhill race against the clock in home-made go-karts at Belchford, a pretty village in the Lincolnshire Wolds. Each competitor free-wheels downhill several times, timed by a stopwatch, and at the end of the day the fastest person or team is the winner. There are many and varied vehicles ranging from the aerodynamic to the novelty entry.

Archie and Emilia hurtled past the starting post, competitors, audience and organisers chasing them on foot. 'YOU HAVE TO WAIT YOUR TURN. STOP! IT'S NOT YOUR GO! STOP!' they shouted.

'WE CAN'T STOP,' shouted Archie as they passed one of the competitors going downhill in their home-made kart.

'That's nice,' said Emilia, looking back at the kart, which was shaped like a vintage car. 'It's a replica of the car in the children's book *Bitsa the Vintage Car and Friends*, I think.'

'Go Archie, go Emilia!' shouted Cindy, Tracey, Jackie and Michelle from the Hambleden Garings Lincoln office, who were stood in the spectators' area. 'Go boss go.'

'Ooh!' shouted Archie as they passed the finish post and careered into the bales designed to stop vehicles with dodgy brakes.

The commentator shouted over the tannoy, 'Brilliant time guys, but I'm afraid we will have to disqualify you for not stopping before the safety bales.'

'Are you all right?' a bruised Archie asked Emilia as they lay upside down next to the lawnmower frame.

'Yeh, fine, you?' she replied.

'I'm just worried that the organisers will get the police out for us jeopardising this event, not to mention stealing the mower at Vernon's. A few bruises are the least of my worries,' said Archie. 'And what have we got to show for it, how can we prove Vernon is up to no good?'

'Well, I took the authenticity documents of the Doge's Diamonds when we left Vernon's, you remember when you were showing off about finding the French door key in the lock and well, Archie, I think now is the right time to tell you, don't worry about the police, you see I am a police officer myself,' explained Emilia.

'I thought there was something shifty about you,' said Archie smiling and winking at her.

They both laughed.

26

Vernon had arrived in Monaco, and gone to the Musée Automobile de la Collection de SAS le Prince de Monaco viewing day. He needed to see the prize Lot – 22 – before the auction itself.

He was pleased to be away from Lincolnshire; he and Rebecca had had a massive row before he left for Monaco. She had carelessly left the signed print he had bought her for her birthday on the chair in the study. It had fallen off and the glass in the frame had broken. Oh the frame could be fixed, but to deny putting the print on the chair – what was that all about? To suggest the house had intruders was also crazy, nothing was stolen; to get the gardener to collaborate her story and insist they escaped on the back of a lawn mower was weird. If they needed a new lawn mower, fine, why bribe the gardener when it was obvious Rebecca had broken the picture frame. What was the matter with Rebecca?

'Or perhaps I over-reacted,' thought Vernon. 'Still, no time to worry about that now, I must deal with things here.'

Vernon still felt uncomfortable about his near escape on the canal in Venice. He hadn't told Rebecca about it. He hadn't told anyone. There was a lot he hadn't told Rebecca. 'Perhaps some day I will,' he thought.

He walked into the viewing area, passing some wonderful

vehicles and automobilia, and casually walked up to Lot 22. What a beautiful vehicle! He looked up at the security cameras placed around the hall and knelt down to look at the car's wheels, which glistened in the fluorescent lighting. 'Truly magnificent,' he thought.

Vernon then departed, timing himself walking from the Bugatti to the main entrance. He made his way back to his hotel. He needed to get some rest – he had a busy night ahead.

27

Auction – night shift

Vernon had set his alarm to midnight. He changed into his security man's uniform and made his way to the Musée Automobile. He checked in with the other security men and took his post in the museum near the Automobile Marques due to be auctioned the next day.

Ten minutes after his shift started he walked up to Lot 22. Vernon could almost smell the petrol as he imagined himself driving the car around the streets of Monaco, just like William Grover would have done in 1929.

Vernon took his mobile from his pocket and using the internet screen was able to log onto a securities site which controlled the security cameras in the museum. He counted the cameras and held the nineteenth camera, which was trained on the Bugatti, on his phone screen. He pressed a code on his phone which meant the camera rotated away from the car. It froze facing the exit. He cut and pasted a shot of the Bugatti onto the screen so the main control office in the museum would see a pre-recorded image of the Bugatti. Vernon was then able to move freely around the car without being noticed.

The car was secured by a sensor beam, so if moved it would alert security – but being a security guard in the museum and also as a result of his somewhat dubious past, Vernon knew how to disable this. He leant underneath the car and pressed the disconnect button. Vernon then took his jacket and cap off, as he had started to sweat. He took his pen out of his pocket and unscrewed it. Inside was the end of a spanner, which attached to one end of the pen. He took the other end of the pen apart to reveal a small screwdriver. He then crawled round the car and started to undo the Bugatti's wheels.

No sooner had he started on the rear wheel than an alarm started to sound, the doors in the display room opened and armed officers rushed in holding guns.

'Freeze!' they shouted at Vernon. 'You're surrounded – don't move.'

Vernon swung the car starter handle and leapt into the Bugatti, dodging the police gunshots. He drove towards the automatic exit door, which dutifully opened. He travelled along the corridor and out of the front doors just before the security shutters dropped down.

The police rushed after him, first on foot down the museum corridors then along the streets of Monaco in their police vehicles, two cars being assisted by a helicopter.

Vernon drove along Avenue Princess Grace, past Le Jardin Japonnaise into Monaco itself, along Avenue Saint Martin and near the palace, back down near the harbour along Rue Grimaldi, up the hill along Avenue Princess Alice and finally turned the corner into Terrace du Casino du Monte Carlo. As he swerved to miss the range of expensive cars in front of the hotel, the back wheel of the Bugatti fell off. The car was flung across the road and landed in the middle of the open air seating area – fortunately closed – outside the Café de Paris. The sun umbrellas and canopies left up from the hot day before came tumbling down on Vernon and knocked him out.

28

Vernon came round a few hours later in a hospital bedroom, surrounded by police. After a few days' hospital treatment – ensuring his accident had not left him too dazed or ill, Vernon would be formally charged. Not only for impersonating a security guard at the museum and stealing an expensive car due to be auctioned, driving recklessly around the streets of Monaco and Monte Carlo, and resisting arrest – but more importantly for hiding and stealing four diamonds of the Doge's of Venice, found in the centre of the main wheel nut of the Bugatti by police investigating at the car crash. These were the very same diamonds Emilia and Archie had found the authenticity documents for – hidden behind the Picasso print Vernon had given to Rebecca for her birthday, encased in the R.J. Langton frame stolen from Lord Armond a few weeks before.

Vernon felt very lonely and very sad imprisoned in Monaco. He was stuck there until the authorities agreed as to where to try him. His wife was also prevented from visiting. He was shocked therefore to receive a visitor – a tall, slim woman in her seventies, greying, but well dressed and still pretty.

He recognised her instantly.

'Hello,' he said. 'It's been a long time.'

'Yes.' She smiled.

'Have you come to help me?' he asked.

'No,' she replied, laughing, 'I want to see you rot.'

Vernon had a second female visitor that same day.

'I didn't expect to see you,' he said.

'I bet you didn't, you bastard,' she said and laughed.

His problems got worse; he found he had to share a cell with a very very angry and violent Italian called Vincenzo.

29

Archie had become quite lucky since Vernon's arrest. He and Emilia had after all played a big part in helping to catch Vernon. They traced the authenticity papers for the diamonds back to Vernon's house. It had all worked out quite brilliantly for him – not only had that dreadful Vernon Hewton gone for good, but Archie was in a position to take over his firm and contracts, which strengthened Hambleden Garings share of the property and professional market in the local area.

Archie had also developed quite a celebrity status since word of his involvement in the arrest of Vernon had been made public knowledge. He had made guest appearances on the *Antiques Roadshow*, *Bargain Hunt* and *Cash in the Attic*. He had also agreed to host a new antiques-based show called *Genuine or Fake?* A celebrity and member of the public would guess whether an item was a genuine or fake antique, a bit like *Call My Bluff*, but with furniture, jewellery and other antiques instead of words.

Lecture tours were also planned. His newly-employed agent Duncan Chambers felt sure a book would follow.

Emilia had her promotion in the police force and the fame she too had earned from the arrest together with her blossoming friendship with Archie made the pair a high-profile celebrity couple — 'ready to rival the likes of Posh and Becks,' thought Archie.

'More like Laurel and Hardy,' thought a jealous Kitty Garings. 'Why couldn't Ronald have realised how dodgy Vernon was? He could have caught him. But oh no, typical Archie comes up smelling of roses yet again. All Ronald got was an invite to open the new town supermarket, as Archie's business partner and then it rained and his car broke down on his way home, something to do with cheap petrol.'

Mr Hambleden senior had done very well out of the arrest also, as the father of the great Archie Hambleden, the man who taught him everything he knew about antiques and bravery. He had made several guest appearances on *This Morning* on their autumn feature, 'Antiques and Crime', and because of his silky voice had become in high demand for voiceovers advertising DIY products, cleaning equipment, furniture, holidays — he was the king of the adverts. He too was hoping for a book deal — *The Voice of Antiques* would be its title. He bought his wife a private plate for her car — after all, as Archie's loving mother she had become quite a celebrity herself and was made Lady Mayor of the town.

'Father,' said Archie 'you can't give mother that number plate.'

'Why not?' said Mr Hambleden 'Its initials and things standing for Benita Isobel Theresa Charton Hambleden, you see the Charton being her maiden name. I changed the Isobel to a double 1, because it's cheaper to form your private plate on the old style number plates, letter, number, number and three further letters.'

'Yes I realise that and I realise you wanted mother's maiden name also, but you've bought her a number plate that spells B 1 1 T C H — I think she may be upset!'

'I see what you mean. I had better rethink, perhaps do something about bees and honey instead. That business of hers seems to go from strength to strength. People just love her honey. It's become a real player in the world of jams and preserves. Our fame has helped promote it further. They say the prime minister even has it on his toast at breakfast time. Loves the taste. As your mother always says, it's all in the way you look after your bees.'

* * *

The Hambleden Garings offices had all been refurbished, and the staff had had a pay rise – the first in three years.

'Oh my boy,' said Mr Hambleden to Archie. 'I'm so proud of you – well done – well done.'

This was praise indeed; normally Mr Hambleden showed very little emotion.

'Father, that means so much to me,' replied Archie. 'It really does.'

'You deserve all the praise, Archie. All this fame and fortune, the dreadful Vernon out of our hair. A high-ranking police officer practically part of the family. Give it a couple of months for the dust to settle and our little smuggling ring can continue, hopefully undetected. The police think they have the main culprit, we will now know if their thoughts change – Emilia will tell you. She doesn't suspect does she?'

'No father – not a thing,' replied Archie.

'Good,' said Mr Hambleden. 'Now tell me once again how you put your brilliant plan into action.'

Part III: Explanation

Email extract . . .

Dear Archie,
Mrs Limb says I'm getting good with this electronic mail
communication system. She says I will soon be a Silver Surfer. I
say I like adventure, but really feel I am far too old for surfing
and as you know I have never been over-fond of the sea.
Your father.

30

As well as being in the property and antiques world since 1833, the Hambleden family had also been diamond and jewel thieves and smugglers. For many years they traded by day respectfully in property, chattels and horses, and by night they robbed the wealthy. They used their auctioneering skills to sell diamonds and jewellery. Very cleverly they would conceal the item of worth inside a lesser item (a diamond ring, for example, in a porcelain bottle with a sealed lid), and advise potential clients of the lot they should be bidding for. Usually there would be little interest in the concealed lot. Money would change hands before the sale.

Although the family identity wasn't known, their supposed existence was the stuff of legend. They were known as the Black Cats or *Les Chats Noirs*. Sometimes they were referred to as 'The Brotherhood of Members', which was the public face of the society, known not for its links with Les Chats Noirs, but as a privileged group for ambitious executives, looking for business contacts and raising money on occasion for charity.

In the 1700s the then Archie Hambleden enjoyed the thrill of being a cat burglar. A mischievous character, he used to leave his calling card at homes he had burgled: a picture of a black cat.

The family secret had been passed from father to son, mother to daughter. The art of jewellery and diamond theft was a way of life. As time had gone on, technology had improved and the Hambleden line had ensured they were up to date with all the latest gadgets. Their extraordinary technical knowledge was however well hidden so as not to cause too much suspicion. To the outside world they appeared very old-fashioned – very twee. After all, the theft of art, antiques, jewellery and diamonds required skill and sophistication, technology and flair. Who would suspect this looking at the Hambleden Garings offices?

Vernon Hewton was no fool – he had technical knowledge himself and felt sure something was not quite right at Hambleden Garings. No firm could be that successful, a family could not have that much money without there being something else. Something more than a two-bit estate agency run on a shoestring. He had already decided that he would try to find out the secret of the Hambledens' success. After all, he wouldn't mind their wealth.

At first Vernon hadn't realised that Archie's family were part of the Black Cat network, but he was alerted to this possibility by chance. His son, young Vernon, had asked him to help him with a school project. Keen to put right some of the mistakes he had made with his daughters previously, Vernon agreed to spend as much time as possible with his son and his project. The project was to investigate myth and legend, a study of historic heroes and/or villains.

While researching on the net and in the local library, Vernon came upon the story of the Black Cats, which he thought might make quite a good project, particularly with the art and jewellery connection. He had an amateur interest in art after all.

He was fascinated to learn about the trading through auctions and the black cat calling card. All in all the Black Cats had been very successful, never caught. Their only failure, as legend would have it, was that they were never able to find the Doge's Diamonds.

The internet article did indeed pose the question, did the Doge's Diamonds really exist? This was a side issue and a further legend that young Vernon could mention in his project, thought Vernon.

'Steady on,' Rebecca had said, 'it's only a seven-year-old's project.'

Vernon's youngest daughter Bambi was studying the history of art at university. He had been discussing the project with her on her holidays from Uni when she gave him some additional information.

Toulouse Lautrec, the famous French artist, had painted *Le Chat Noir* in poster form. This image was the same one used on the smugglers' calling card. A pleasing design, it could also be found on T-shirts, caps and handbags on the Continent. In fact, Bambi had a postcard of the design which she had bought from the National Gallery shop when she went on a lecture trip there the previous term as part of her course. Furthermore, the cat's eyes in the poster shone very brightly and legend suggested that they resembled diamonds.

Archie, Vernon had thought, when Bambi presented him with her postcard of *Le Chat Noir*, had that very print on his office wall, an auctioneer himself and . . . 'Oh my God, his cat is black, it's called Lautrec! Is there a link? Is this the secret of the Hambledens' success? Their fortune?'

Vernon just knew he had to investigate things further. If Archie was part of the Black Cat network imagine what it would mean for him if he were to uncover the truth.

Vernon knew Archie Hambleden didn't like him, but with the cattle market partnership he knew he could perhaps get on side with some of the staff and over time even be able to gain Archie's friendship and possibly trust. Vernon was very good at gaining people's trust, a proper charmer.

31

Who Was Henry Stanley?

The television programme, *House Hunter*, provided Vernon with a lot of business success and on the back of that he had been contacted by Henry Stanley, the chairman of the International Association for Museum Awareness. He was invited to talk to some of the organisation members in Venice: with his experiences in estate agency, the preparation for the television programme and his own interest in paintings – Picasso's work in particular – he should be an entertaining after-dinner speaker.

Henry Stanley was a tall, dark-haired chap of Italian descent and worked in the Museo Correr, Venice. His own particular field of interest was antique stones and art of the Renaissance period. His particular fascination was with the Doge's Diamonds and the history surrounding them. His wife Monica was Dutch and a professor in diamond studies. Henry arranged the sale of some jewellery for Vernon on his trip to Venice. Vernon was to bring the antique necklace, earrings and watch with him to Venice and Henry would value the items for him and possibly arrange a sale. The jewellery had been left to Vernon's son, in a family will. The will stated that Vernon should either keep the jewellery or sell it, either way the items or proceeds should go to his first-born son on his eighteenth birthday.

When Henry Stanley had personally telephoned him to invite him to Venice, knowing his knowledge of diamonds and jewellery, Vernon could not resist asking him for a valuation. He then sold the jewels to a friend of Henry's, a private Venetian collector. He made fifteen thousand pounds in cash, so felt sure he could save eight thousand for his son, which, with interest over eleven years, would make him a nice nest egg. The remaining money and his fee for talking to the museum guests would go a long way to a swimming pool at home and, after all, young Vernon would also get the benefit of this.

Henry became a good friend to Vernon and arranged many more lectures for his organisation in Venice, Rome and Paris, to name but a few locations. Knowing his expertise in diamonds and his fascination with the Doge's Diamonds, Vernon told Henry about his concerns relating to Archie and together they came up with a plan to try to catch Archie out, assuming he really was involved with the Black Cat network.

However, Vernon didn't realise that Henry himself was a Black Cat and he and Archie were in fact planning to set him up instead.

32

Methodology

Archie knew Emilia was a police officer from the beginning. The police had been getting dangerously close to finding out the truth about the Black Cats. He needed to try to send them on a false trail.

Vernon was a pain and he also needed getting rid of. More recently Vernon had started asking questions about the business. Archie felt sure he fancied himself as a private detective and came up with a plan to set Vernon up. For a while at least that would get the police off his patch.

Vernon was a rotter, and he jumped at the chance for a free valuation on his son's jewellery. The prospect of a cash sale, no tax, also appealed to him. The elaborate carrying of bags and tubes provided ideal visual clues to Emilia when they followed Vernon to Venice. Particularly as Vernon carried some of his lecture prints in a tube which looked like it could house the Picasso print.

Archie fell into the canal in Venice on purpose, so as not to be spotted by Vernon and to coordinate things with Henry. He suffered quite a cold as a result of this and felt quite humiliated, but he would do anything to protect his business interests.

Regular trips abroad for Vernon were assured, and Henry coordinated these. Vernon was so egotistical he would believe that his sudden rise as a successful speaker was a direct result of his appearance on *House Hunter*. Of course Henry Stanley, during a visit to London, would watch the programme and consider that all his troubles finding new and interesting speakers were over – Vernon Hewton to the rescue!

The Picasso print and frame was a gift to Vernon from Hambleden Garings. Vernon and Archie liked to gamble and Archie lost a poker game to Vernon (on purpose – which hurt), but being gentlemen they didn't bet for money, that would be too crude – they gambled for goods. A signed Picasso print was Vernon's prize. It would make an extra gift for Rebecca on her birthday, but Vernon also put it in the *House Hunter* programme house, to show it off and piss Archie off even more. Not only had Archie lost to him at poker, but his signed print was also lost, and having it displayed all over the TV, well, Vernon couldn't resist showing off and rubbing Archie's nose right in it.

Archie stole the R.J. Langton painting and frame before the fête and auction at Armond Hall. Mr Hambleden senior had convinced Lord Armond to withdraw the painting from the sale. They had purposely sent it up and down the country through the auction houses to try to flush the inspecting officers out of the woodwork. To have R.J. Langton's great-great granddaughter inspecting the case made it the perfect bait.

Archie removed the painting from the frame and replaced it with the Picasso print, then prepared his video for him and Emilia to replay the *House Hunter* programme and check out the frame. Vernon had now been implicated in the burglary. Archie knew Emilia would try to inspect the painting at Armond Hall, so he had to steal it before she got there. This made him, and Mr

Hambleden senior, late for their auction at the fête. Nevertheless, Emilia was well and truly set on the trail to find the painting, the frame, and Vernon. Shame Lord Armond shot her up the backside, but luckily for her he was a rotten shot, so it wasn't as serious as it could have been.

It had been a nice touch to send Vernon to Venice, the home of the Doge's Diamonds, on a lecture, with details of how to set up the Black Cats. Looking at Vernon's recent vigorous travel record, the police would want to know why. After-dinner speeches seemed a bit far-fetched – and Venice was key.

The director of the *House Hunter* programme, also a Black Cat, organised the programme featuring Vernon in double quick time, which helped set the double-cross in motion.

33

The Doge's Diamonds

Giovanni Bellini painted a portrait of Doge Giovanni Mocenigo in 1480. He had been the official portrait artist to the Doges of Venice from 1474. This particular portrait depicts the Doge's ceremonial dress. It is now located in the Museo Correr, Venice.

The Doge's Palace can be visited today, and it looks very grand next to the beautiful St Mark's Basilica. It is a fourteenth-century gothic palace, and was the seat of government for the former Venetian Republic and the residence of the head of state – the Doge.

On great occasions and in processions the Doge was followed by all his insignia and badges of office. On his ceremonial dress he had six diamond buttons – the Doge's Diamonds, which were passed from Doge to Doge and were always worn on the ceremonial dress.

It was no easy matter defending the Doge and legend has it that in 1492 insurgents stormed the palace and stole the ceremonial robes. The robes were never seen again, but the diamonds forming the buttons were traded on through the black market.

Diamonds are a gemstone and are recorded as far back as the

thirteenth century. At this time they were only worn by royalty. They are hard and optical. They cannot be broken or worn down. This meant that they were difficult to trade in past times without trace, particularly the six famous Doge's Diamonds.

It was not until the nineteenth century that society high-flyers started to wear diamonds and trade became easier according to carat (weight), cut and colour. The Doge's Diamonds, stolen many years before, had been hidden after all, not traded as first thought.

Restorers found the diamonds hidden in St Mark's Square, Venice, in the bells of the *Campanile* (the great bell tower). The diamonds were authenticated as the Doge's Diamonds by the Museo Correr and displayed in the Basilica of St Mark. They were red, rough cut and very rare; worth around fifteen million pounds or more, per diamond. Unlike platinum, gold or silver, diamonds do not carry a hallmark. The assessment of the quality and value of any diamond used to be down to the knowledge and integrity of the supplier, and experts of the day were convinced the six diamonds were in fact the Doge's Diamonds stolen centuries before.

The Black Cats wanted those diamonds.

During the Carnival in 1806, the masked party which still sweeps through Venice every February, the diamonds vanished. There had been a small fire in the Basilica and in the confusion of the carnival and the flames of the raging fire in the Basilica, the diamonds were removed. The authenticity papers were all that remained.

34

Henry Stanley, with the help of his diamond expert wife Monica, had researched the history of the Doge's Diamonds and had made it his life's work to try to trace their whereabouts. He had finally found four of them hidden in the wheel hubs of a Bugatti racing car in Monaco, or so he told Vernon Hewton. It was this discovery and Vernon's concerns which made him decide to help Vernon catch the Black Cats. If Archie was involved, Vernon would have the added pleasure of seeing him go to prison for a long time and possibly be able to take over his business. Henry Stanley would finally see four of his beloved diamonds restored to their rightful place in Venice – the glory for the Museo Correr and him personally would be very great. In fact, both men would reap great rewards.

Of course, Henry being part of the Black Cat smuggling ring, was in fact working with Archie to set Vernon up. Both men devised an elaborate plan to trick Vernon into being found in possession of the diamonds.

The Black Cats had in fact stolen the Doge's Diamonds centuries before in the fire at the Basilica, as previously described. Due to their reputation the diamonds had to be hidden for many years. The Black Cat descendants were made aware of their whereabouts, ready for them to reappear on an appropriate monetary-rewarding occasion. Archie and Henry felt that the time had come to aid the discovery of at least four of the six diamonds.

35

Lot 22 – The Bugatti

Four of the diamonds had been found in the Bugatti in the Marque Auction in Monaco. The Black Cats had hidden the diamonds there to set Vernon up. Why Monaco? Well, some of the diamonds were already hidden there, so they did not have to be smuggled over the Italian border – also there is approximately one policeman to every sixteen houses in Monaco and a sophisticated CCTV system in place all over this tiny country. So it would near enough ensure, in the right circumstances, that Vernon would be very publicly arrested. With the Grand Prix connection and the fame Monaco has for high society living, Archie and Henry felt that this would be the ideal location to finally remove Vernon from their lives.

Also, the fact that senior officials in Monaco were Black Cat members served to aid Archie and Henry's cause.

Henry told Vernon that the numerous *ridotti* (clubs) in Venice in the 1800s hosted gambling groups and were full of card sharps. The main *ridotto* near St Mark's was a kind of Monte Carlo and belonged to the Dandoli family who also had casinos, clubs and real estate businesses in Monaco. Rumour had it that members of the club were also Black Cat members and after the fire in St Mark's some of the Doge's diamonds made their way from there to the club with a little bit of help from a Black Cat or two. Smuggled out of Venice by travelling actors and entertainers, who were popular among society high-flyers, the diamonds were almost undetectable among the fancy dress costumes.

The diamonds eventually reached Monaco and had been hidden in the casino belonging to the Dandoli family ever since, secreted in one of the chandeliers made in part of Murano red glass.

Four of the six diamonds, Henry told Vernon, were later stolen from the Black Cats by a disgruntled ex-member and lost until the Monaco police, the senior officer being a good friend of Henry's, discovered them in a safe in an abandoned flat.

Only recently had the Monaco police discovered the diamonds and established their authenticity, therefore the news of the find still had not been made public knowledge. Keen to catch the Black Cats, the senior police officer agreed to set Archie – widely believed to be a senior, if not *the* senior Black Cat – up.

Through a contact in the underworld, Archie would be notified of the diamonds' discovery and prior to making the find public knowledge the diamonds would be protected. On the day of the automobile auction, with all the press in place, the find would be revealed to the world.

Why use the Bugatti? Why make a big to-do about the find?

'A fitting conclusion to a mystery that has baffled many for centuries – the ideal way for Monaco to show off its discovery. Brilliant,' Henry had told Vernon.

In fact, all Black Cats loved vintage cars, the Bugatti being a particular favourite. Until recently this Bugatti had been on display in the Dandoli family casino in Monaco.

The idea was that if Archie knew about the diamonds he was sure to try to retrieve them. Vernon, as a security guard, together with the full back-up of the police, would be ready to arrest Archie at the museum. It was Archie who should have been driving the Bugatti, not Vernon, the night Vernon was arrested. But Archie didn't show. Vernon had disconnected the security camera, as instructed by Henry. He said the Monaco police did not want the auction security team to jeopardise their grand capture.

When the police tried to arrest Vernon following the surprising alarm activation in the museum, Vernon panicked; he felt sure his innocence would be confirmed if he could just get to the Monaco police headquarters, and contact the chief of police and Henry Stanley. Both men suddenly developed amnesia.

'I have never heard of anything so ridiculous,' Henry Stanley had said. 'To think I trusted this man Vernon, he even talked about art to myself and my colleagues at various lectures.'

36

When Archie and Emilia discovered the verification documents for the diamonds behind Vernon's Picasso print, Vernon's fate was well and truly sealed. Henry Stanley quickly confirmed that the papers were genuine.

'The British police, following an intensive round of questioning Rebecca, contacted the Monaco police and the rest you know,' Archie said to his father.

'Yes,' said Mr Hambleden, 'I knew all the efforts I went to, dressing as a friar and all the courting Carlo Dandoli did with that receptionist, that Maria, at Museo Del Duomo, in Castello, back in 1972 would pay off one day. That Pinturichio painting of the Madonna and Child was lovely, I would have liked to have kept it.'

There was a knock at Archie's office door and in walked Emilia.

'Hello,' she said. 'How's my two favourite auctioneers?'

'Very well dear,' Mr Hambleden replied. 'I will leave you two young celebrities alone.'

He left the room.

'Do you fancy a holiday?' Archie asked Emilia. 'I think we have earned it.'

'Yes Archie, that would be good,' she replied, 'but first tell me where the other two missing Doge's Diamonds are hidden?'

The blood drained from Archie's face. 'You know?' he gasped. 'But how? I mean . . . oh my God.'

37

The two remaining diamonds

Lincoln cathedral towers over the city of Lincoln, the capital of the Wolds. This historic religious building is considered second to none among appreciators of religious buildings. The cathedral is built of stone quarried out of the ground on which it stands – thus externally it displays a honey-coloured limestone, internally there is much marble on display.

In 1548, the steeple on the central tower, made of lead sheathed timber, crashed, and later, in 1807, the smaller steeples on the western towers were taken down.

A record of all who have worked on the cathedral is kept in the minster library. One of the men working there during 1807 was a Mr Archibald Hambleden.

Legend has it that Satan sent an imp to Lincoln cathedral to cause trouble. The imp was destroying the angel choir when an angel appeared, but the imp jumped up onto a pillar and started throwing rocks at it. The angel then turned the imp to stone, as he is today in the cathedral. The imp is now well recognised as a symbol of Lincoln and Lincolnshire.

Few people realise that there are in fact two imps, one inside the cathedral and one outside. There are many stories written about the imp legend, and one expansion on the basic story just told is that there were in fact two imps. The first was turned to stone; the second is said to have escaped with the help of a witch. The imp went off with the witch on a broomstick, but the witch was so fond of him she wanted to keep him as a pet, and decided to turn him into a black cat to keep him safe.

Recent visitors to the cathedral will remember the second imp with witch and broomstick was covered in a sock while repair works were being carried out. Sadly, frost damage to the outer imp's head meant full repair was required. Interestingly, the damage by frost caused at the beginning of 2005 was far more severe than before, but then Archie had inherited his ancestors' talent for masonry and an interest in buildings. The outside imp, a black cat, was a pretty good place for Archie's ancestor to hide the missing two diamonds.

R.J. Langton, himself a keen academic with an interest in the Black Cat organisation, had been commissioned by the Black Cats to paint Lincoln cathedral, depicting the whereabouts of the remaining two diamonds. The outer imp was on full display in his painting. It was the perfect map. Ownership was the perfect symbol to the Black Cat organisation of a person's background.

Of course the diamonds were now safe with Archie, the Toulouse Lautrec print of *Le Chat Noir* in Archie's office fitted over the R.J. Langton painting perfectly. The diamond-shaped eyes of the Black Cat on the print itself had just a little bit more sparkle than previously.

*   *   *

'So now you know the location of the missing diamonds, are you going to arrest me?' questioned Archie. 'Or . . . Of course, how

123

stupid of me, you're R.J. Langton's great-great-granddaughter, you would know the story of the diamonds and their whereabouts, and you wanted the diamonds for yourself, that's why you cried at the auction. Are you going to rob me? Perfect, steal from a thief, no comeback.'

'Rob you, or arrest you, Archie Hambleden? Difficult to say, perhaps neither. I have a good career and yes the diamonds will be a nice pension fund, but I am prepared to share.'

'What about Vernon, I mean, I can understand you wanting the best of career and money, but don't you feel a little guilty about Vernon? I mean it's different for me, I hate him.'

'So do I, Archie,' replied Emilia 'So do I.'

'But, well I mean why?' asked Archie. 'You have no real reason to − do you?'

'Oh Archie I do, believe me I do,' replied Emilia.

Part IV: The Future

So, I thought as I was passing through Lincoln to do a survey, I would take the opportunity of popping into the paint shop to get some cans of paint for the auction house store room. Duly loaded into the boot, I was alarmed to hear a rolling sound as I turned the corner into Monks Road. I pulled up, and thinking that the lid may have come off a can of paint as it was rattling around the boot, I lifted the boot lid and was mildly concerned to note that as the lid rose, the paint can took an effortless swallow dive onto the road – whereupon it immediately exploded in a shower of bright orange paint all over the road, my shoes and lower trousers.

Placing said open can on a rag on the floor in the passenger side of the car – thereby getting more paint on the carpet and door trim, I continued to the golf club room, where, in anticipation of meeting someone at my next appointment, I tried to wash my trousers free of paint. Of course, to start with, when you add water, the paint spreads ever more thinly and young Archie, you would be best to remember, should you have a similar unfortunate episode, that the only way to look anything decent, which of course is not what happens, is to soak said trousers in copious quantities of water. Now, you being young, it wouldn't matter, but when you get to a certain age you do feel slightly vulnerable to thoughts that people might be thinking 'poor old git – he's wet himself', so when you do meet someone you tend to go into verbal diarrhoea and start prattling about exploding paint cans and the like. Which is worse – being accused of incontinence or senility?

Your father.

38

'Vernon Hewton was once my mother's business partner,' said Emilia. 'He stole money from her and endangered her life. It nearly destroyed her. She has never been quite the same since. I think Vernon has paid back some of what he owes my mother now, don't you?'

'But, what do you mean?' questioned Archie, feeling quite shocked but at the same time intrigued.

'My grandfather on my mother's side, as you know, was a descendant of R.J. Langton. My mother met my Italian father at university and went to live with him in Italy soon after they were married. My father wanted to return home to Umbria. My mother was an estate agent and for several years lived happily in a place called Città di Castello. When she fell pregnant, for a long while she didn't realise she was expecting twins. When myself and my brother Leo arrived, my mother just couldn't cope with running the estate agency on her own and looking after two children. Sadly my father developed a gambling habit, he lost a fortune, turned to drink and drugs and indeed became very violent. He never really worked.

'His family were wealthy landowners. They bailed him out of debt on numerous occasions, selling the odd estate house here and there. Eventually they disowned him though. Vernon James Hewton (known as James in those days) lived for several years in Castello; in fact he worked for my mother in her estate agency for a while and became a rock to her when my father turned violent. He basically ran the firm for a while, allowing her to devote as much time as possible to Leo and me. Vernon, though, wanted to take over the estate agency as his own; his plan was to buy it from my mother at a rock-bottom price. So he encouraged my father's gambling habit, unbeknown to my mother at the time.

'When my mother planned to leave our father, she confided in Vernon. He arranged to buy the estate agency from her and send the money on to England. In those days you didn't leave your husband lightly in Italy. My father would have never have let my mother take Leo away – he was his precious son, the continuation of the Fizzelli name. She had no choice but to escape. We all three left Italy; following months of secret meetings our Black Cat connection smuggled us out. I remember being very scared, I dread to think how my mother felt. Our start in the UK was very difficult. I think my mother wondered on occasion whether she had made the right decision to leave Italy. Our life in Italy was quite comfortable. I can't eat turkey now, the smell of the cargo train we took to get to Rome will be with me for the rest of my life, in fact I can always smell it, my mind playing tricks of course, when I am scared or nervous about something.

'Just before we were due to leave, my mother had been to her office to pick up various legal documents she had hidden away from my father – he never went to the office, you see. As she was leaving a fax arrived for Vernon, who was not about; it confirmed how his money would not be transferred to my mother when she arrived in England as he had instructed. Because of the circumstances of our escape my mother had a difficult choice to make – we stay, fight Vernon, and risk spending a long and

128

miserable life with my father, beating my mother up, taking drugs, gambling, or we escape as planned with nothing.

'We couldn't just leave in the car, everyone knew my mother, she was very blonde and didn't look Italian at all. My father's family at that time still supported him, he was still their precious son who could do no wrong. It wasn't until much later that they disowned him. My mother was unusual in Italy at that time, a successful businesswoman, a foreign lady to them and unlike Italian women she said exactly what she thought. My mother is very nice, a lovely person, but she calls a spade a spade, you know exactly where you stand with her. It earned her much respect and custom in her estate agency business and friendship from her staff, she was always very fair. It could on occasion land her in hot water with Italian bureaucrats and officials. I remember one time she dared ask the local priest, who Papa's family had invited to the house for tea, a great honour indeed for such a devout Catholic family as they were, whether the story of St Francis of Assisi, one of the most beloved and famous of the Italian saints, was altogether true. She wanted to know whether he really did receive the stigmata from Christ as legend reports when he was praying on Mount Verna, or whether in fact he inflicted the wounds himself to his hands, feet and chest, to feel pain and feel closer to God, and ensure his place in history. Which of course it did.

'Early accounts of St Francis after all suggested he sought pain for himself and would sleep in discomfort to demonstrate the strength of his religion. Her argument was that if stigmata was given in love from a holy source, why did St Francis die only two years after, likely from his weeping wounds? The priest could not answer this and was quite cross and dismayed that anyone should dare question the legend of St Francis. This caused a scandal at the time. Mama wasn't being disrespectful, she just likes to know the reason behind things, she is very intelligent and told the priest

129

she felt there were often ordinary explanations for these so-called miracles.

'With my mother's "fame" among some locals, if I can call it that, it was very necessary we leave in secret, as it was highly likely the Italians would always support my father despite his obvious terrible behaviour towards her and the envy and business respect she did in fact have with the locals. At the bottom of it, although they accepted her and indeed liked her, she wasn't Italian and she was a woman doing a job expected of a man. So Father being a big strong, wealthy Italian man, in the locals' eyes, when really looking back he was weak, sad and insecure, would always get their first loyalty.

'My mother has always put my brother and me first. Leo and I have worked hard to ensure we have achieved success in work to thank mother for the risks she took and sacrifices she made for us. Leo took his middle name and I altered mine into an English form from Millia to Emilia. I took the surname Langton, but Leo used a distant uncle's surname as he was most vulnerable, being the son and heir, it was important we were not traced and snatched. Now there is no problem of course. In fact I believe our father is in Monaco, a guest of the principality along with his old friend Vernon. I guess they will have a lot of catching up to do.' She laughed. Then, turning serious, she continued.

'In the beginning life in England was hard, as I have just said, in fact we had to buy our clothes from charity shops. My mother came from a good background and our new lifestyle was very different. It was a real shock for her, but she got back on her feet eventually, working in estate agency firms, first as a viewing consultant, then a negotiator, eventually middle management in a large chain of estate agents in London. In fact I went to see her after our trip to Venice, and she then went off to Venice herself and nearly killed Vernon. She had a gun and everything.

130

'Thank God my brother caught up with her and calmed her down. I think she fired the shot, and regretted it when it was too late, the bullet had left the gun, but fortunately it just missed Vernon.'

'Gosh,' said Archie, quite stunned, 'I had no idea, none at all, I mean I knew you were a police officer and you . . . well I mean, you told me you had a brother, but you didn't say he was a twin or tell me you history. You naturally must be very close to your mother and brother having gone through all that together. Does your brother live in London also?'

'No my brother lives in Venice; in fact Archie, you surprise me,' said Emilia. 'Don't you recognise the family resemblance – I know we are not identical but I mean to say, Henry Stanley is my brother.'

'Bloody Hell!' replied Archie. 'I had no idea, he's always been a good friend, God I thought I knew everything about my fellow Black Cats, guess I was wrong. Father always tells me I must never take my eye off the ball, God knows what he will think of this.'

'Our secret, Archie,' replied Emilia, 'if you don't mind, old wounds and all that.'

'OK, understood,' said Archie.

'Anyway, well done, you certainly stitched the bastard up, still a lot of trouble to go to in order to get rid of the competition,' said Emilia. 'Mum did go and visit Vernon in prison, she said he was a broken man. Those who say revenge is overrated are wrong, she said it was such a relief to finally get even with him, some sort of justice. I can understand our motives, but what are yours? I hope you don't mind me asking, I know your art and diamond trading is rather dubious to say the least, but you don't come across as vicious just for the sake of it. Let's face it, what you have done to Vernon is vicious, brilliant, but vicious.'

39

'My mother visited Vernon in prison in Monaco also,' replied Archie. 'She must have been in the country at the same time as your mother. Mum is a wheeler-dealer and she was . . . erm, let's just say wheeler-dealing tobacco in the 1970s in Umbria and learning the Italian language. When the lovely Vernon was there working with your mother, he burgled the house she was staying in, in the Niccone valley. She was looking after it for some old friends while they were away. Vernon appeared at the foot of her bed, surprised the house was occupied. It traumatised her, she had a lot of trouble sleeping for ages and then wrote to the authorities in Italy. She recognised Vernon's piercing eyes, that stare of his, immediately when he returned to Lincolnshire. He stole a gold brooch from mother, a cat with diamond-studded eyes, that father had bought her, which added to her distress. We Black Cats always look after our own and will always get revenge. The Bugatti was a good publicity stunt, it ensured media attention. My father had for many years had the Doge's Diamonds authenticity papers hidden in a specially created hollow section of its starter handle. It was on display in the Dandoli casino in Monaco. So when we retrieved the stored documents, it was quite a fun idea to use the Bugatti again, only this time to house some of the diamonds. To have the stolen authenticity papers on such public display for so long and get away with it, appealed to my father's sense of humour. To then use the same vehicle for the diamonds just seemed so right. You are quite right, revenge is really a lovely feeling.

'Thankfully, now my mother has also been able to get over the terror of Vernon and of course she's been able to throw herself into her honey business; that's really taken her mind off things. It's going great guns.'

'Erm,' said Emilia, 'I need to speak to her about that. Her honey is a favourite of prime ministers, kings, queens, and even the president of America raves about it.'

'Oh,' said Archie quite sheepishly, 'do you want some honey?'

'Now, Archie, cross-pollination bees and those pretty cannabis plants in her garden may help prime ministers and presidents rule the world, but, as a police officer there are only so many blind eyes I can turn.'

'Can't you turn one more blind eye, just one more for your future mother-in-law?'

'Archie Hambleden, what are you saying?' blushed Emilia.

'Well, put it this way,' said Archie, 'if you don't agree to marry me under your own free will, I will feed you pots and pots of mother's honey until you are that high you'll agree to anything.'

They both started laughing.

40

'Nice young Archie seems to be getting settled with that Emilia girl,' said Mr Hambleden senior to his wife Benita.

'Yes, I am pleased,' she replied, putting her newly-returned gold brooch of a cat with diamond-studded eyes on her bedside table, just below the painting recently purchased by Mr Hambleden hung on the wall of *Dora Maar Au Chat*. 'Now come on dear, try to get some sleep, you have a television interview in the morning.'

There was a short pause.

'Archibald, Archibald! Listen, listen!'

'What are you shouting about, woman?' said Mr Hambleden, 'you've just told me to get some sleep, now you're squawking and have woken me up.'

'I can hear voices in the study!'

'Oh God, we've got intruders!' said Mr Hambleden. 'Right, leave it to me.'

Mr Hambleden got out of bed, picked up his walking stick and moved to the door, followed closely by Mrs Hambleden, complete with hairnet and rollers.

The couple crept downstairs.

'They're definitely in the study,' whispered Mr Hambleden.

'Do be careful Archibald, you're not as young as you were, I hope it's not that horrible Vernon back with those piercing eyes!'

'I'll sort it dear, once a Black Cat, always a Black Cat,' Mr Hambleden replied as he launched at the door with his walking stick raised.

'Stop right there, thief!' he shouted as he pushed the door open.

In the corner of the room, plugged into the mains on charge was his satnav system. It kept repeating, 'You have reached your destination, you have reached your destination, you have reached your destination . . .'

'Oh Archibald, for goodness sake, that bloody satnav,' said Mrs Hambleden.